Lost Horse

GLENN BALCH

Lost Horse

ILLUSTRATED BY PERS CROWELL

FAMOUS HORSE STORIES

GROSSET & DUNLAP

Publishers, New York

To

Edith Garrison Balch

*a mother who always understood
a boy's love for horses*

Lost Horse

Lost Horse

CHAPTER ONE

V INCE DARBY and his boys were branding calves in the big corral that lay on the flat between the house and Crystal Creek on the day that Tom Sample, the horse-runner, came back to Tack Ranch. Vince Darby never refused anyone a meal or a place to sleep, but for two years Tom Sample had not been welcome at Tack, and Tom Sample knew it. Vince Darby was a blunt, plain-spoken man, strong in his likes and dislikes, rigidly just, and not given to compromising.

On that bright June afternoon all the Darbys were at the big corral—all, that is, except Milly, more affectionately called "Mom." Milly was even then taking a cake from the oven of the big cast-iron range in the square kitchen of the ranch house. That kitchen and the house were Milly's domain and she left the running of the ranch to Vince and the boys.

The one on the horse, a lean wiry youth just well into his teens, was Ben. Ben had lank, yellow hair, a well-fleshed face, and long arms and legs, and he sat on his horse with unconscious ease and assurance. The flanker was Steve, wide shouldered and big handed, four years older than Ben and now practically a man. Dixie tended the branding fire. Slender and straight, with freckles across her tilted nose and hair the color of new wheat straw, Dixie wore boots and levis and blue shirt like her brothers' and, because of her marked preference for outdoor activities, was commonly considered "one of the boys." Although she was two years Ben's junior, there were few things about horses and cattle that she didn't know and couldn't do.

Vince Darby stood at the branding fire on his sturdy, slighty bowed legs and knew a contentment in the easy, skillful manner in which the work progressed. A haze of fine dust mingled with the blue smoke above the pen. Fat, white-faced calves crowded in one corner, blatting their uneasiness. The cows, held in a smaller nearby corral, bawled their anxiety through the openings in the rails. Steve's horse dozed under the saddle and at trailing reins near the fence.

Ben's job was to catch the calves, which he did by riding among them and tossing his rope with a sure, smooth motion. He then turned his horse and brought the lunging and bawling calf to a place near the fire. Here Steve took over. Grasping the taut rope, Steve went along it, hand over hand until he reached the calf. Grabbing front leg and flank and putting his knees firmly against the calf's fat side, Steve gave an expert lift and push that flipped the little animal's feet from under it. When the calf hit the ground, Steve fell on it like a wrestler and quickly squirmed to a position behind it, where he could grasp the upper hind leg in both big hands and brace his boot against the hock of the lower leg. In such a position, with Ben's horse leaning firmly against the neck rope, the calf could do little but bellow and bawl.

Then Vince took an iron from Dixie's fire. When Tack stock was being branded, nobody but Vince handled the iron. Vince was proud of the brand, which was the outline of a big-headed, short tack. It had to be placed just right, on the big muscle of the animal's left shoulder, and at just the right angle, burned not too deep but just deep enough to leave a lasting mark. There could be no question about the brand a Tack animal wore. The iron was shaped somewhat like a potato masher, and the brand itself was on the downward face. Vince wore heavy leather gloves because the long metal handle sometimes became uncomfortably hot. Holding the glowing metal above the calf's shoulder, Vince said, "Hold him still, Steve," and squinted along the handle as if he were aiming a gun. Then he lowered the iron to the hide and leaned his weight against the handle, watching the sharp little curl of acrid smoke come up from the burning hair. The calf bellowed and struggled, but Steve, at the tail, hung on tightly, knowing full well that if either his hands or his foot slipped there would be some fast and furious kicking. But even worse, his father's aim might be spoiled. This would result in a smeared brand and would cause the elder Darby to frown whenever he saw it.

After he had made the brand, Vince handed the iron to

[3]

Dixie to be taken back to the fire and nestled among the glowing coals. Then Vince took out his knife. The blade was bright and sharp. Vince always handled the knife too. Kneeling beside the calf, he castrated and earmarked with quick sure movements, then took the can of disinfectant from Dixie and liberally swabbed the wounded parts. When everything was completed to his satisfaction, he said, "All right, Ben," and waited till Ben stepped up his horse to slack the rope so that he could take the noose from the calf's neck. As Vince stood up, Steve released his hold and rolled quickly out of the way. The calf scrambled to its feet and galloped across the corral to the others, crowding in among them for comfort.

Out of school at Boise less than a week, Ben knew a great pleasure at being back among the familiar sounds and smells of the ranch. He was ranch raised, and this was the life he loved, riding horses and working with stock. He had a strong feeling for horses and cows; he liked the fast, absorbing work in the branding pens and the breaking corrals; he liked the freedom and the satisfying vastness of the big Owyhee country sky and the long ridges and draws and the upland basins. And especially he liked the high Twin Buttes country where the wild horses roamed in keen-eyed bands led by the proud stallions.

Ben thought to himself as he pulled in his rope coil by coil, that one of these days soon, when the branding was over, he would ride up there and have a look. The wild horses would be back now, back from the wintering range in the Owyhee breaks, and they would be fat and sleek and

[4]

full of fire from the strong summer grass. There would be new colts, frisking at the side of their mothers; the colts he had watched the year before would be yearlings now, growing up into horses, young and strong and as wild as the antelope that shared the range.

All these thoughts were running through Ben's mind when he looked up and saw Tom Sample standing at the corral fence. Tom Sample was a tall man, with a rider's narrow, high-shouldered body. He had little gray eyes set in a loose-featured face. He wore a horseman's garb: boots, whipcord pants, plaid flannel shirt, and soft felt hat. The boots were fancily stitched, with white inlays in the shape of hearts and diamonds, and his belt was wide, hand carved, and had a big silver buckle with the figure of a man riding a bucking horse—a flashy symbol of the man's trade. It was a handsome outfit, but it didn't impress Ben—not on Tom Sample. It was a Sunday cowboy's rigging, and besides, Ben didn't believe that Tom Sample was made of the stuff that makes a real bronc-rider.

Such business as Tom Sample had, however, was horses —buying and selling, training and trading. He had a barn and corrals in Caldwell, and he followed the rodeos. Many horses passed through his hands, going to pleasure riders, ropers, and bulldoggers, even to the professional bucking strings, generally with a profit to Tom Sample. He was shrewd and had acquired the reputation of being a good judge of horses, and he was always eager to turn a dollar.

Ben knew there was trouble in the offing when he looked up and saw Tom Sample standing at the corral fence; knew it better than ever when he saw the cheerful grin on Tom Sample's face.

There had been a time when Tom Sample had been greeted in a friendly manner at Tack, when he had been welcomed to a place at the table and a bed in the upstairs bunk room where Ben and Steve slept. But that was before the summer that he had brought Pearly Maunderland and two other horse-runners to Twin Buttes to try to catch the black stallion. The Darbys had learned then that Tom Sample was greedy, cruel, and selfish.

Tom Sample saw in the black stallion a powerful, ferocious horse that would be a big drawing card in the rodeo arenas, a horse that through brutal treatment could be turned into a fighting outlaw that would earn him many dollars, so Tom determined to have the animal and he put his riders on the black's trail. But to Ben and Dixie, King—the name they had given the stallion—was a proud, glorious symbol of the high country's freedom, a fine sire that would increase the quality of the wild bands and deserved to live out his life as the leader of his kind. They hated the thought too of the taunting and cruel treatment that he would receive as an arena outlaw. Having watched the big black as he roamed the high country and having even given him a name, they felt also a priority interest in him, a kind of absentee ownership and therefore they set out to prevent the horse-runners from getting him.

They caught the stallion themselves and branded him with the Tack mark. Then they freed the wild horse to go back to his band, for they loved King and respected his desire to be free. Tom Sample knew that neither he nor anyone else would dare put his hand on a horse carrying Vince Darby's Tack brand. So on that summer afternoon, two years before, Tom Sample had ridden away from the ranch on Crystal Creek in a glowering rage, knowing that he had been frustrated by a boy and a girl, and would never have the beautiful, wild stallion that he had sworn he would possess.

Ben looked again at that smile on Tom Sample's face and knew there was trouble. Tom Sample had neither forgotten nor forgiven, but here he was back again, as cheerful and as sure of himself as if the summer of two years ago had never been. Ben's nerves tightened and their ends tingled uneasily. He looked at Tom Sample without a sign of recognition, but Vince, noticing Ben's intentness, raised his head and looked toward the fence.

"Hello, Vince," Tom Sample said pleasantly. "Those are good-looking calves you're putting your brand on."

Vince straightened up and walked over to the fence. "What do you want, Tom?" he said. "What are you doing here?"

Sample's smile stiffened slightly and he said, "I just dropped by, Vince. I want to talk to you about a horse."

Vince eyed the man sharply for a few seconds, then said, "I've got no horse to talk to you about. I won't sell any horses to you, Tom; you know that."

Sample shook his head. "I'm not trying to buy horses this trip. It's a question of ownership. Or maybe it's Ben's horse?"

"Is it wearing a Tack brand?"

"Yes."

"Then it's mine," Vince Darby said. "And there's no question of ownership."

"Maybe not," Tom said, "but at least you can talk about it. There's no harm in that, is there?"

Vince was undecided but he was a civil man, with a determination to be fair, and he said, "No. But just now we're busy."

"I'll wait," Tom Sample said.

Vince turned back to the corral and nodded his head at Ben. Ben sent his horse, Inky, into the bunch of calves and put his rope on a big strong one, four months old. He turned Inky to the fire and liked the way the calf fought and plunged against the rope. Steve caught the calf and turned him down easily, and Ben knew that Tom Sample was seeing a good crew at work. Ben found pride, too, in the steady unruffled manner in which Vince applied the hot iron. But he couldn't shake his feeling of anxiety.

While Inky leaned against the rope, Ben let his eyes wander to the area behind Tom Sample and saw, up near the house, a long, heavy car. That, he decided, was the way Tom Sample had come. But this nettled him still further, for he knew that Tom Sample never owned a big, expensive car. When he looked more closely, he saw that there was a man sitting quietly under the wheel. Who was he? And what did he want? Why had he come with Tom Sample to Tack? Ben didn't know, but he was very sure that he wouldn't like the answers to his questions. The presence of the car and this strange man added, in Ben's quick imagination, to the trouble he was certain Tom Sample had brought.

"Okay, Ben," Vince said. Ben stepped up his horse and his father threw off the loop. Ben pulled in his rope as he rode into the calves. He quickly made a small noose and dropped it over a white-faced head. When he turned Inky around he noticed that the smug smile was back on Tom Sample's face, and it annoyed him to think that Tom was laughing at them.

The gaucho came riding out of the willows that lined the creek. He was a little, brown man with black hair, eyes, and beard. He sometimes dressed outlandishly in bright sashes, baggy pantaloons, and soft low-heeled boots, and he always wore a little, brown, full-crowned hat that sat jauntily on his thick hair. He was quiet, shy, and usually smiling, but occasionally he carried a knife—a facon, he called it—in the sash at his back with the handle conveniently close to his right hand and he could, Ben knew, draw and throw that knife with movements so swift that the eye could not follow.

The gaucho had come to Tack that exciting summer two years before. Confused, uncertain, struggling with a strange language, he had, on some impulse or whim, asked Vince, in the Caldwell sales yard, for a job of breaking horses, and Vince, encouraged by Ben, had taken him on. He wasn't as tall as Ben, but stockier, and he had many strange ways, but above all he could handle horses. He didn't "break" horses; he "made" them, made sensitive mouths and agreeable willing dispositions. He developed steadiness and obedience; he instilled trust and confidence. If a colt had any good in him, Gaucho's training would bring it out.

So Vince Darby had kept the gaucho, had kept him after he had refused to build fence, put up hay, help with the branding, or do any of the many chores that were necessary around a ranch. Gaucho was a horse-trainer and nothing else, and after Vince had ridden one of the colts Gaucho had trained, Vince was satisfied to keep him at Tack. With his happy disposition, his innate kindness, his pride and strong sense of loyalty, the South American had become much more than just a hired hand during his two years on the ranch. He had won a permanent place in the Darbys' affection and was treated as a member of the family.

The gaucho was riding a blaze-faced, bay colt and he headed the animal toward the round, high-walled, breaking pen, which was his particular domain. But his keen eyes saw Tom Sample standing at the branding corral and, with sudden decision, he reined the bay in that direction. He rode up and drew the colt to a halt a few feet from the horse-trader.

"Hello, Gaucho," Tom said.

"Hullo," the gaucho answered, but there was no friendliness in his voice. He was remembering that summer two years before when Tom Sample had accused him of stealing a horse, had called him a "spic" and a "pepper belly," and had threatened to have him arrested.

And Tom Sample was remembering the speed with

[10]

which the little man produced a knife from nowhere and hurled it when Pearly Maunderland was in the act of pulling a gun.

Vince Darby felt the tenseness in the air and looked up and said, "It's all right, Gaucho. Tom just dropped by to check on a horse."

"Is it Listo?" Listo, a sand-colored mare, had been in the string Tom Sample had brought to the high country to run the black stallion, but Gaucho claimed that she was his, brought by him from his native pampas and stolen at the big Pendleton Roundup. And Gaucho, with characteristic directness, had taken her. Later, in the face of Tom Sample's anger, he had proved to Vince Darby's satisfaction that he spoke the truth. Vince knew that Sample had never forgiven him for taking the gaucho's side in that.

Ben heard the quick belligerence in the gaucho's tone and, knowing the deep affection the brown rider had for the mare, knew that he would never give her up—not even on a sheriff's orders, if that man waiting so quietly in the big car were a sheriff.

Tom Sample said, "No, it's not Listo, Gaucho."

Over by the fire, Dixie got to her feet. Forthright and unabashed, she stood in awe of no one, not even her father. She moved over and confronted Tom Sample. "What's all this?" she said to him. "What have you got up your sleeve, Tom Sample?"

"Dixie," Vince said.

"What is it?" she said to Tom. "I'm tired of all this mystery stuff. What's on your mind?"

"Why . . . why nothing," Tom Sample said. "I just—"

"Let's have it," she insisted. "What horse are you talking about? Which horse do you want to check on?"

"Why—" Tom said, somewhat disconcerted—"why, that black stallion, up in Twin Buttes."

"King?" Ben cried sharply from his saddle. "You haven't got any claim on that horse, Tom Sample, and you know it. He's Tack. I put the brand on him myself."

"The Listo mare had a Double-Deuce on her," Tom Sample said. "That's Johnny Crutcher's brand, down in Nevada."

"What's that got to do with it?" Vince demanded. "Listo was stolen. Johnny Crutcher never owned her. You know what the law is with regard to stolen horses."

Tom Sample nodded his head, with a satisfaction so obvious it was irritating. "Yes," he said, "I know. I ought to, I've just been looking it up."

Vince glared at the man a long minute, trying to guess what was in his mind. Then Vince turned back to the corral. "Hurry up, boys," he said. "Let's finish branding these calves, so we can turn them out and find out what Tom's got on his mind."

CHAPTER TWO

THE MAN sitting in the automobile was not a sheriff. His name was Andrew Blair and he came from Arizona, where he owned a big breeding stud, specializing in fine racing horses. Tom Sample introduced him after the branding had been finished and all of them, even the gaucho, had trooped up to the house.

"I am glad to know you, Mr. Darby," Andrew Blair said, offering his hand.

Vince nodded and shook hands, while his eyes under their thick brows studied Blair closely.

"Nice place you have here," Blair said, glancing around at the green fields with their tight wire fences.

"Yes," Vince said.

Blair was a middle-aged man, with a strong, sober face and good, level eyes. He wore breeches and high English boots that, while well polished, showed strong marks of narrow stirrup leathers. Ben knew the man was accustomed to riding flat saddles.

"I've never gone in much for cows," Blair said. "I've always raised horses."

Vince nodded and said, "Yes." He was still waiting for the man to bring up the subject of the visit. Tom Sample was standing back, letting Blair do the talking. But that mysterious smugness was still on Tom's face.

Ben had been prepared to dislike Andy Blair, but now, looking at the man and hearing him talk, he found it difficult. Blair was not bombastic or overbearing or antagonizing; on the contrary, he was friendly and unassuming. But Ben, like his father, still had his guard up. He would trust no friend of Tom Sample's.

"I suppose you are wondering why I'm up in Idaho?" Blair said presently.

"Yes," Vince said.

"I'm on the trail of a horse," Blair said. "It has been a long trail and, until a few weeks ago, a cold one. Perhaps it still is, I don't know. But maybe you can help me."

Vince hesitated, just noticeably. "We'll do what's right," he said.

"I'm sure you will," the Arizona man said. "And, of course, I expect to pay you for any trouble you might have gone to or that I might cause you."

"We'll see about that," Vince said. "What about this horse you're after?"

Blair turned to his car and took some pictures from the glove compartment. He glanced through them, selected one, and handed it to Vince. "Did you ever see that horse before?" he asked.

[14]

Ben quickly squirmed around so he could look past his father's shoulder. He saw a picture of a tall, powerfully built, dark animal, standing in a proud, high-headed pose, without saddle or bridle. The horse had on a halter, the shank of which was held by a man standing out of the picture. There was an indistinct, white building out of focus in the background.

Ben's heart leaped in his throat. It was King. But that was impossible, this man couldn't have a picture of King. No, it wasn't King. It looked like King, but it wasn't. King's body was shorter; not much, but just a little; and King was heavier through the neck and shoulders.

"That's not him," Ben said huskily at his father's shoulder. "That's not King."

"No," Vince said to Andy Blair, handing the picture back. "No, I haven't seen that horse. I don't know him."

Blair took the picture, turned it so that he could look at it, and a sad expression came into his eyes. "Did you ever hear of Midnight Fire?" he said presently.

"Midnight Fire? Of course," Vince said. Everyone interested in horses in the country had heard of Midnight Fire, the famous racer.

"He's dead," Steve said. "I read in the papers that he had died, four or five years ago, as I remember."

"Longer than that," Andy Blair said. "Yes, Midnight Fire is dead."

"That's his picture," Dixie guessed shrewdly. "You owned him?"

"For a little while, just before he died," the man said. "I saw him race and I wanted him for a sire."

"He was a hard-luck horse," Tom Sample said. "He was pushed through the rail at Tia Juana and hurt his leg."

"It wasn't too serious," Blair said, "but it prevented his racing any more. The men who owned him weren't breeders and they agreed to sell him to me. I believed that he could transmit his fine qualities to his colts, so I took him to my stud."

"But what's all this got to do with us?" Ben asked, irritated by his anxiety.

"You'll see," Tom Sample said.

"I don't know," Andy Blair said. "Sample here thinks there might be a connection, but frankly I'm dubious. It's a long shot, but certainly worth following up. It is something of a long story too. I got three colts from Midnight Fire."

"Only three?" Vince Darby said.

"Yes. Less than a month after I got him to my ranch he was dead. It was one of those tragic accidents. He was a high-spirited, strong-willed horse. On the race track he never admitted that he was beaten. He would run his heart out first. That's one reason he proved to be such a great track horse. It wasn't speed so much as it was determination. I believe he was the most determined horse I ever knew."

The man's description caused Ben to think of King—high-spirited, determined, and fiercely proud. He would run until he dropped before he would let the horse-runners get close to him.

"What happened?" Dixie said.

Andy Blair smiled at her as she stood slender and boyish in boots and levis. "You love horses, don't you?" he said. "Well, it was a little thing, or it seemed to be. A new man I had working for me tied Midnight Fire in his stall one night, tied him to his manger with a strong rope. Midnight hated to be tied; he hated anything that restricted his freedom. He even hated to be shut in a stall, but during his track days he got used to that. Still at times he would paw against the door, seeking to get out in the paddock. We always kept him in a high solid-walled pen, where he could get plenty of fresh air and exercise, but couldn't see out. The sight of other horses caused him to become highly excited."

"Most stallions that are kept up are like that," Vince said.

The Arizona man nodded. He paused briefly before he went on. "It was really my fault. Midnight's former owners warned me against tying him up, and I had given orders that he was always to be left loose in his stall, but this new man didn't know that, and I didn't think to tell him. 'Didn't think' is a poor excuse, especially for a man who handles livestock. Animals don't think. When they are running loose their instinct serves them well, but when we men start controlling them we have to think for them. This new man didn't know and he wasn't smart enough to ask. But

[17]

there is no use finding fault now; Midnight Fire is dead."

"He killed himself," Vince guessed.

"No, he wouldn't do that," Ben said.

"The rope, it would no break," the gaucho said, nodding his dark head wisely.

"No," said Tom Sample, "but Midnight Fire's neck did."

"Yes," said Andy Blair. "He was dead when we found him the next morning. He had practically torn the manger apart. But it held long enough to kill him."

"But . . . but . . ." said Ben. "Why did he do it?"

"Little things sometimes make a big difference to horses," Andy Blair said. "I have known a mouse running across a stable floor to throw them into a panic."

"I've had them shy at their own shadow on a moonlight night," Steve said.

"When they're in a panic they may go crazy," Blair said, "especially if something hurts them. Midnight burned and bruised his front legs fighting that rope."

"Gee, that was too bad, to lose a good horse like that," Dixie said.

"I believe he was the best sire I ever had," Blair said.

"But what's all this got to do with us?" Vince Darby said. "We raise stock horses, not racers."

"I'm coming to that," Blair said. "As I told you, I got three colts from Midnight Fire. Two were fillies and the third one was a horse colt. Under the terms by which I acquired the stallion, the former owners were to have their choice of the first crop of colts."

"And of course they took the stud colt," Steve said.

"No, they took one of the fillies."

Steve shook his head. "For racing, I'd rather have the horse."

"They would have too, but the horse was not available. They took a filly out of a thoroughbred mare called Fly Away. The filly's name was Fire Fly."

"Fire Fly?" Vince said. "You don't mean . . . ?"

Blair smiled. "That's her. She's burning the tracks. Hialeah, Santa Anita, Hollywood, Tia Juana—she has won all over the country. She's a chip off of the old block. Here," he turned and went through his photographs again, "here's her picture." It was a trim, slender mare under a racing saddle.

Looking past Vince's shoulder, Ben said, "She's a beauty."

"She shows speed," Steve said.

"It seems to me I've seen her before, there's something about the way she carries her head," Dixie said, frowning in an attempt at recollection.

"You've seen one that looks a whole lot like her," said Tom Sample.

"Who?" Dixie said.

Tom did not answer but grinned, and Ben did not like that grin. It had something leering and evil in it.

Vince Darby handed the picture back. "Go on," he said to Blair. "What about the stud colt?"

Blair went through his pictures again, selected one and handed it to Vince. "That's Warrior's Queen," he said.

The Darbys gathered around Vince to view this new picture. Warrior's Queen was obviously a brood mare, with a big, well-sprung barrel but with the fine slim legs and the head and neck of a thoroughbred.

The pucker between Dixie's level blue eyes deepened.

Ben took the picture to look at it closer before handing it back to the Arizona man.

"She had a good track record and was the best of the lot," Andy Blair said. "She was still racing when I bought her. I especially wanted to mate her with Midnight Fire."

"Did you?" Vince said.

"Yes. She had the horse colt."

"What happened to him? Where is he now?"

"I wish I knew," Blair said. "One morning Warrior's Queen was gone from the pasture, her foal with her."

"Gone?" Vince said. "What happened to her?"

Blair nodded. "We tracked them to a section of the fence that had been taken down, then tracked them to the tire tracks of a car and trailer. We followed the tire tracks to the main highway, which was hard-surfaced. They turned west. That was as far as we could follow them."

"But Mr. Blair," Vince said, "how does this concern us? There's hardly a horse on this ranch that we haven't raised ourselves, except Keister. I had him sent out from Kentucky. Do you want to look at him?"

"Yes," Andy Blair said. "I always want to look at good horses. But later. Let me finish about Warrior's Queen and Midnight Chief first."

"Midnight Chief?" Dixie said.

Blair nodded. "That's what we named the foal. He was nearly a year old when they disappeared, and a handsome colt. I had already refused some good offers for him, but I didn't even consider selling him. I raise horses to sell, but you see, Midnight Fire was dead and this was his only horse colt. I wanted to keep him to carry on the strain. He looked a lot like his sire. And of course, the former owners had first claim on him. I was hopeful that, if they took him, they would let me buy him back."

"But the rustlers got him first?" Dixie said.

"I'd call them horse thieves," Blair said. "But that's another thing that made it bad. The former owners suspected, I believe, that I had conspired to get the colt out of the way before the time arrived for them to make a choice. You can see the position this put me in. I've been raising and dealing in horses all my life and I value my reputation for honesty and fairness."

"They thought you were hiding the colt out on purpose?" Steve said.

"Well, they didn't say so—not in so many words. Eventually they took Fire Fly, and I know they are well satisfied now. But I'm determined to clear the matter up and, too, I wanted to recover Warrior's Queen and her colt if possible. I circulated the mare's picture all over the country—you've probably seen it somewhere, Miss—and hired detectives at all the big tracks. I was pretty certain she would show up at the races, for she was well known and still a comparatively young mare."

"He found her, too," Tom Sample said.

"It took seven years," Blair said, "but we found her. Her mane had been clipped and her tail cut short, and I guess she had been dyed a time or two to disguise her. But one of my men recognized her, at a race track down in Nevada."

"What about the colt—Midnight Chief?" Dixie asked.

Blair shook his head. "He wasn't with her, which was not surprising, since he would have been about eight years old then. A man by the name of Thurman was racing her. I had never seen or heard of him before. He said he bought her from a man by the name of Larkness in Colorado. We started tracing back. Larkness had bought her from a man in Wyoming, who had found her in a cow outfit. Finally we came to a man by the name of Selkins, who couldn't account for the manner in which she came into his possession. We took him back to Arizona, where he was convicted of horse-stealing and sent to prison. Then he confessed."

"He was the one who stole her?" Vince said.

"Yes. He and a companion, who knew Queen's track record, planned to steal her and campaign her on the small northern tracks. They only wanted the mare, but they found that they couldn't load her in the trailer without taking the foal too. So they put both of them in, covered the trailer, and headed for the state of Washington, traveling at night and hiding out in the daytime. Of course the mare had to be watered and fed, and they traveled the back roads to avoid attention. The colt was difficult to handle and they realized that keeping it made them more likely to be detected. They became frightened, even considered shooting the colt, but finally compromised by turning it loose one dark night in the rough country. As near as Selkins could remember it was somewhere near the point where the Idaho, Oregon, and Nevada boundaries meet."

"That's wild country," Tom Sample said.

"Yes, I know," Blair said. "I've been there. It's broken and rough, not a fence or a house for miles."

"They left that little colt out there?" Dixie said.

"That's what Selkins said. And, since he had already been convicted, I see no reason for not believing him."

"But he might have died," Dixie said.

"He might have," Blair agreed. "I wouldn't be too greatly surprised if he did."

"But he didn't," Tom Sample declared.

"Tom seems to be pretty certain that he didn't," Blair said. "I hope he's right, but it seems almost too good to be true. To find Midnight Chief again, after all these years— I can hardly believe it. And now of course he will be mine, since the former owners took Fire Fly."

Vince Darby turned to Sample. "What makes you think he's still alive, Tom?" he said.

"Tom believes he found a band of wild horses and has been running with them," Andy Blair said. "He thinks he has been running with the wild horses all these years."

Vince Darby shrugged. "That might be, Mr. Blair. But I don't see how it concerns us. We don't pay much attention to wild horses around here—that is, I don't. I've got a good Kentucky stud that gives me better colts than I can get out of the wild bunches."

Ben spoke up then. "Some of them are pretty good," he

said stoutly. "There're some good colts with the wild bunches that run up in Twin Buttes. Remember Inky, Pop? Remember my Christmas Horse? He came right out of a wild bunch."

"Yes," Vince admitted. "But where you find one like him, you'll find a hundred that are worthless. Isn't that right, Mr. Blair?"

Blair smiled. "I don't know whether I should mix up in any father and son controversy, but I would say that most of the wild horses I have seen are not worth much. Really, considering the feed they get and the hardships they undergo, you can't expect much of them. Two or three generations of that and no wonder they are stunted and scrawny."

"But not all of them," Ben said. "There's some good feed up on Twin Buttes, and the rocks give them good hard feet and make them quick and sure footed."

"Say, Mr. Blair," Tom Sample said suddenly, "come down to the corral with me. I want to show you something. It's all right with you, isn't it, Vince?"

The elder Darby might have denied the request to Tom Sample, but he felt that he could not be rude to Andy Blair. "Yes," he said.

Tom Sample, important and sure of himself, led the way to the branding corral, with the rest of them trooping in wonderment behind him. The calves had been turned out and, with their mothers, were wandering away from the area, but the two saddle horses which Ben and Steve had used were still standing to trailing reins inside the dusty enclosure.

Tom Sample stopped at the fence, put one fancy boot on the lower rail and waited until they all arrived. "See anything, Mr. Blair?" he said. "See anything that looks familiar?"

Ben, puzzled, looked up at the Arizona man and saw that Mr. Blair was staring at the dark horse with wide eyes. "That's Inky, that's my horse," Ben said, not without a touch of pride. With Johnny Horn, the roping champion, riding him, Inky had proved himself the year before to be a top arena horse.

"See anything, Mr. Blair?" Tom Sample said again.

The Arizona man seemed to have heard neither Ben nor Tom Sample however. He kept looking at Inky. Presently he spoke. "That head, those shoulders—" He whirled to Tom Sample. "That's Midnight Fire breeding. I'd swear to it." He turned to Ben. "Where'd you get that horse?"

"But . . . but it can't be," Ben said. "Inky is a wild horse, out of the wild bunch. King is his sire."

"This King horse, I want to see him," Blair said.

Ben was too confused to speak.

"He's a wild stallion," Vince Darby said. "He runs with his bunch up on Twin Buttes."

"There," Tom Sample cried. "What'd I tell you, Mr. Blair?"

"But he's mine," Ben cried. "King is mine."

"Yes, he is," Dixie said firmly. "We caught him and put our brand on him. He's Tack. Tom Sample knows that."

"Stolen," Tom Sample said. "He's a stolen horse."

"He's not," Dixie insisted.

[25]

"If he's your horse, I won't bother him, Miss," Andy Blair said. "You can be sure of that."

"At least . . . at least, I don't think he's stolen," Dixie said, shaken in her confidence.

"Aw," Vince said, "there's not a chance in a hundred—not one in a thousand."

"According to range law, the man who puts his brand on a wild horse owns him," Ben said. "That's the law."

"But not a stolen horse," Tom Sample said. "Remember, the Listo mare had Double-Deuce on her, but that didn't make her Johnny Crutcher's."

"Not one chance in a thousand," Vince Darby said.

"Show your picture, Mr. Blair," Tom Sample said. "Show them the picture."

Andy Blair thumbed through his photographs again and handed Vince a picture of a mare and a colt, taken in a grassy pasture with a grove of trees behind and a white rail fence in the distance. Ben crowded against one side of his father and Dixie craned her neck on the other side. Even Steve moved closer, where he could see. It was the mare Warrior's Queen, undoubtedly. And the foal, gangly legged and short bodied, a big, dark, high-headed colt, was King. Even in the immature head, the neck, and the long sloping shoulders Ben could see the wild stallion, just as Tom Sample had undoubtedly seen him when Andy Blair had shown Sample the pictures in Caldwell.

Tom Sample, knowing the store Ben and Dixie set by the big black horse and still stinging from his previous defeat in an attempt to catch King, had to have his minute of triumph. "Speak up, Ben," Tom taunted. "Do you know that colt? Ever see him running with the wild bunches up in Twin Buttes?"

Ben couldn't speak; his heart was choking him. He and Dixie and the gaucho had saved King once, had saved him for the wild band which he so superbly led and which needed him so badly as a sire, had saved him for the high, rugged country that needed proud, spirited stallions. Ben had felt secure in that Tack brand, knowing that neither Tom Sample nor any rancher would dare touch the horse. But now— No, no, something cried out inside him. Say it isn't King; it can't be. King was a wild horse; he was not born in a deep grass pasture. Not King. King was a horse of the rimrocks, of the dry, dusty sage, of the rolling hogbacks and long distances. King was a horse of the winds and the rains, of the thunderclouds and the downpours, of the canyons and the river breaks. No, no— but Ben could not get words past the mighty lump in his throat.

CHAPTER THREE

SUPPER was over at Tack. The boys and the gaucho had washed the dust from their hands and faces and had slicked down their hair. Dixie had changed her levis for a fresh, yellow-figured dress which, in the lamplight, matched her hair. Their mother, finished in the kitchen, came in with a basket of socks that needed darning. Vince had on his glasses and sat in his rocker, close to the lamp. The *Stockman's Journal* was in his lap, but on top of it was the picture of a mare and her colt.

Vince picked up the picture and studied it closely for a minute. There had been no discussion of it at the table and all of them knew that the time had come for the matter to be threshed out. "You always claimed that that horse had no ordinary breeding, Ben," his father said presently.

"Yes sir," Ben said, wishing now that he had not been so positive about it.

"You're pretty certain this is the one?"

"Well, I couldn't be sure of it. It looks like him, but of course I couldn't be absolutely certain."

"I know, but if you had to say 'yes' or ' no,' which would it be?"

"I guess I'd say 'yes,' if I had to say," Ben replied unhappily.

"Here, Dix," Vince said, handing the picture to the girl. "Which would you say? You've seen the stallion often enough."

Dixie took her time in answering. She had been as determined as Ben that the big horse should stay in Twin Buttes and had played an important part in catching him. "I'd say it might be," she said, "and then again it might not. There are a lot of horses that look alike, and it is pretty hard to tell what a yearling colt is going to look like when he's seven or eight years old. I would say that Mr. Blair would have to have better proof than just this picture."

"Isn't there any distingushing mark, like a white foot or something, that would show in the picture?" Mom said, slipping the darning egg into a sock.

"No," Vince said, "not a thing. They're both solid color. This picture is not too clear anyway."

"There's a mark on King," Dixie said, "a big Tack brand on his left shoulder. That means a lot to me."

"Sure," Ben said, backing her up. "He was a wild horse —and we caught him. There wasn't a brand or saddle marks or anything on him. He was a wild horse and we caught him and put our brand on him. That's good enough in this country."

"Usually, yes," Vince admitted.

"But if this horse was stolen from Mr. Blair, then he

wasn't really a wild horse," Steve pointed out. "Someone owned him. It wasn't Mr. Blair's fault that he got away."

"He was running with the wild bunch," Ben said doggedly. "Why didn't Mr. Blair put his brand on him?"

"They don't usually brand race horses and horses that they never expect to turn out," Steve said. "In some sections you see a lot of horses that aren't branded."

"That's his hard luck, not ours," Dixie said. "I'm not going to give King to just any man who comes along and claims him, especially not if he's got Tom Sample with him. Tom Sample has been after King ever since the first time he saw him. I wouldn't believe Tom Sample on a bet."

"I wouldn't either," Ben said.

"I guess Mr. Blair doesn't know Tom the way we do," Vince said. "He probably just ran into him by accident, trying to find somebody who knows about the horses in this country. And Tom saw a chance to get even with us. But that's not Mr. Blair's fault. He's just trying to find his horse. You can't blame him for that."

"Well, I wish he would get someone else to help him," Dixie said.

"That's not our business," Vince replied. "All we've got to do is to determine whether King is the colt he had stolen from him, if we can."

"If he is, what're we going to do about it?" Ben said. "We've had him longer than Mr. Blair did. We've got a better claim to him. He's been wearing the Tack brand two years now."

"Yes," Vince agreed. "But if he was a stolen horse, then

[30]

we had no right to put a brand on him in the first place."

"I don't see how Mr. Blair can prove it." Steve said. "Colts change a lot as they grow up."

"If it's his horse, it's his horse," Vince said. "The breeding strain shows up pretty strong in a lot of horses."

Ben nodded in agreement. "Remember what he said about Inky? He said Inky was Midnight Fire breeding. And King is Inky's sire. You only have to take one look at them to know that. But gee, Pop, you know yourself that a lot of horses look alike."

Vince Darby handed the picture to the gaucho, who had been an interested listener but had taken no part in the conversation. The South American rarely spoke unless first spoken to, perhaps because of his broken English. "What do you think, Gaucho?" Vince said. "You've had plenty of opportunity to see the black stud. Is this the horse?"

Gaucho took the picture, glanced at it briefly, and said, "Si, señor."

"But, Gaucho, how can you be sure?" Ben said, taking the picture and studying it for the twentieth time. "There isn't a mark on this colt."

Gaucho shrugged. "Is the other picture, the big horse," he said.

"Which one? Midnight Fire?"

"Si. Is the poppa—how you say it?—the sire."

"King's sire?"

"Si."

"But how? How can you tell?" Ben said exasperatedly.

"Es verdad. The head, the shoulder, the—how you say it?—carry—it is the same."

There was no doubt in the gaucho's mind and a gloomy silence followed his statement. Milly didn't look up from the sock she was darning. Vince took up his magazine, opened it, and pretended to read. They had reached a decision which they had hoped to avoid and beyond which none of them was prepared to go just then.

Steve got up and stretched and said, "Guess I'll go to bed." He went up the stairs and they could hear his boots clunking across the bunk-room floor above them.

The gaucho was quiet and still on the worn leather sofa. He knew what he had done and his brown face with its thick black beard was sober and thoughtful.

Ben knew he was not sleepy, and he didn't want to play checkers with the gaucho. Dixie was fiddling with the radio, but Ben didn't want to listen. He wanted to get out of the house, away from everyone. "Guess I'll go down and have a look at Inky," he said, and added lamely, "he might want a drink."

He went through the big kitchen, now neatly cleaned up for the night, out the back door, across the porch with its shelf and washpans and down the steps. The moon had not yet come up but the night was clear. The smell of sage was fresh and strong.

Ben moved along the hard-packed path. Inky was in the barn, in one of the open stalls. But tonight his mind was not on the dark, little roping horse, and before he reached the barn he turned to the right, moving on, until he came against the worn gray juniper rails of the branding corral. He stopped here, hooking his elbows over the top rail. The wind stirred the white ashes of the branding fire and beyond the opposite fence the fringe of dark willows swayed gently.

Ben did not blame the gaucho; the little rider from the pampas was merely being honest, as was his nature, and Ben would not have him any other way. But he felt that Gaucho could have been less positive about the matter. Gaucho knew how much store Ben and Dixie set by the black stallion, knew how determined they had been to keep him up in the high country. Gaucho had even helped them catch the big horse; without Gaucho and his Listo mare Ben knew they never could have done it. It was Gaucho who threw King and tied him up, so Ben could put on the Tack brand, using a hot cinch ring held between two sticks. Gaucho had helped them from the first; he knew the whole story. Yet without hesitation, Gaucho said the black stallion was Andrew Blair's stolen horse. And what really annoyed Ben was that the gaucho's simple certainty had settled the matter in Ben's own mind. The big black horse which he and Dixie had named King, after watching him leading the bunch and fighting the other stallions, was really Midnight Chief. He was not a nameless wild horse but an aristocrat, carefully bred, by the mighty Midnight Fire and out of Warrior's Queen. This fact awed Ben. King was a blueblood such as Ben had scarcely dared dream about. And Inky was, too. Inky was old Midnight Fire's grandson, which might account for his fine showing in the arena.

But Ben was more concerned with King. It seemed so unfair that they should lose him after all the trouble they had had to catch and brand him. They had been honest about the matter; they had believed he was a wild horse and they had saved him from Tom Sample. If Tom Sample had caught him, he would have been worth nothing by now, worn out in the rodeos, even if he were still alive. Ben was sure of that. He and Dixie had saved King.

Also, now that he knew King's background, Ben felt more than ever that the stallion should stay up in the high mesas. His breeding was just what the wild bands needed, to build them up and improve the quality of the individuals. In a few more years there would be as good horses up there as anywhere in the country. No one could call them scrubs and broomtails after that. And this, Ben thought, would be the perfect breeding, the infusion of purebred racing blood with that of the hardy range mares. What colts! Ben's eyes gleamed at the thought of them— strong, rugged horses with speed and power. Yes, and beauty. Sure footed and quicker than any thoroughbred. The miles they would carry a man! He thought of Inky. A better horse than Inky had never looked through a bridle, in Ben's opinion. And, in Ben's opinion too, horses like Inky, real working horses, were more important than high-strung racers. As he stood there by the branding pen under the soft gleam of the Owyhee country stars, Ben Darby had no trouble convincing himself that the black stallion was vastly more important as a leader of the wild bands than he would be on an Arizona breeding farm.

A soft step sounded behind Ben and he turned to see Dixie coming, as the breeze tugged languidly at her short-cut yellow hair. "Oh, it's you," Ben said, turning back to the corral, somewhat annoyed by the ease with which Dixie could sense his moods and thoughts. On occasions such as this he pretended to tolerate her, though secretly he admired her outspoken frankness, especially with Pop, and valued her loyal partnership in almost every project that he undertook. Of course, however, because she was a girl, and being younger, she had to be kept in her place.

Dixie came up to the fence, hooked her arms on the top, and placed one foot familiarly on the lower rail. Then, with characteristic directness, she went right to the heart of the matter. "It won't seem right up there without King," she said, raising her stub nose toward the canyon rim beyond Crystal Creek. "Up there" was Twin Buttes, with its brush and rocks, its basins and hogbacks, its ridges and arroyos.

Bitterness welled up in Ben. "It won't be right," he said. "King belongs up there. The wild bunches need him."

"Yes," she agreed. "You can already see the difference in the colts."

"I'll say you can," Ben said. "Look at Inky; he's the best horse in southern Idaho. Of course, there won't be many like him, but they'll be good horses. They'll be stock horses, something a man can do work on, not just fancy racers that have to have a track as smooth as a kitchen floor."

Dixie agreed with him. "I wouldn't give five cents for one," she said.

"I'd be afraid to ride one, in this country," Ben said. "I'd be afraid he'd fall down and break my neck."

"He wouldn't last a day in the rocks," she said. A gloomy silence that lasted more than a minute followed, and then she said, "We ought to do something about it."

That idea had been in Ben's mind too and it brought a pertinent question which he now put into a single word, "How?"

She considered this, then said, "I don't know, but there ought to be something. We kept Tom Sample from getting him."

"Yes, but that was different."

"Well, there ought to be some way," she said. "Maybe Mr. Blair can't catch him," she added hopefully. "He doesn't know anything about wild horses. I'll bet he can't even get close to King."

"He couldn't," Ben said. "But he'll get Tom Sample to do it for him. That's what Tom's hanging around for. Tom'll get Pearly Maunderland and Axil Pickett and maybe another man or two, and they'll use grain-fed horses and relay King till he can't walk. That's the way they tried to do it before. Only . . . only, this time we won't be able to stop them. There won't be a thing we can do about it, and Tom Sample knows it. That's what he's so happy about."

"You think Tom'll do it?" she said.

[36]

"Sure, and old Blair will pay him good money for it. He's a sucker, but he doesn't know it yet."

"He'll find it out, if he hires Tom Sample," Dixie said.

"Yes, but what good will it do then?"

"Oh," said Dixie, "I wish Pop would tell Tom Sample to stay out of Twin Buttes."

"He can't do that. Twin Buttes is open range. Anybody can go up there who wants to. We could keep them from coming across Tack land, but it would be easy to go around."

"But there must be something we can do," Dixie insisted. "Maybe we could go up there and run King back so far they couldn't find him. Maybe we could run him back across Butte Creek Canyon. He could hide in the breaks."

Ben shook his head. "It wouldn't do any good. Even if we could get him across the canyon, he would be back on his old range in less than a week. Tom Sample would find him."

"If we could catch him, we could hide him out," she said. "We could keep him in that old corral at Little Butte. There's water and we could take hay up for him. They might not look there; they wouldn't think about it. And when they're gone we could turn him out again."

That idea had possibilities and Ben turned them over carefully in his mind. Tom Sample's riders might spend weeks up there, even all summer, without going into that grove of trees where Ben had found the old corral. And they could easily fix it up to hold King, especially if they kept him on a long rope for a few days to get used to the place. And they could put another horse in there to keep him company, an old gentle one. They could pack up the hay at night, so Tom Sample wouldn't see them and guess what they were doing. Tom would see the wild bunches, but he wouldn't find King and he wouldn't know what became of him. And after a while, Tom would give up and Andy Blair would go back to Arizona. It might work, Ben knew, and it was the only thing he could think of that had much chance. It would be hard work for him and Dixie, but they would not mind that. They would have to get the gaucho to help them, however, for it would be a big job to catch King, and Gaucho was the only one they could really depend on. Pop would not help; Pop had no time for wild horses. And he wouldn't let Steve help them.

A third figure came along the path from the house and turned down to the branding pen. It was the gaucho. He came on and presently stood beside Ben at the fence. He wore no hat and his thick, dark hair ran past his ears and down into his neatly cropped beard.

Each lost in sober thought, they leaned there for several seconds, then Ben said, "Will you help us catch the black stallion again, Gaucho?"

"Si, mio amigo," the man said. "I will help."

"We're going to keep him," Dixie said.

"Remember that corral in the juniper grove?" Ben said. "We'll put him in there."

The gaucho saw the whole plan immediately and nodded, indicating that, in his opinion, it might work.

"The question is: can we catch King quick enough, before they see him?" Dixie said.

Ben had doubts about that too. "He'll be hard to catch; you know how long it took us to run him down before, even after Tom Sample had been running him. But we can try." He looked to the gaucho hopefully for suggestions, knowing that the rider had had much experience in running wild horses on his native pampas in South America.

The gaucho considered the matter, then suddenly shrugged. "What is use?" he said. "El Señor Darby, he will no—how you say it?—stand for it. It is horse of el Señor Blair. For interfere, Señor Pop will no permit."

That was a fact both Ben and Dixie had been trying to dodge, for they knew that it was the heart of the whole matter. That was their father's way: what was his was his, positively and emphatically, and he had the same uncompromising respect for what belonged to the other fellow. If their father was convinced that the black stallion belonged to Andy Blair, then he would not turn a hand to prevent Andy Blair from having possession of the animal, nor would he permit anyone else on Tack to do so. Unable to get around this fact, Ben had been merely ignoring it. Now he could do so no longer, and he had a deep feeling of helplessness.

"Darn!" Dixie said. "Why does Pop have to be so stubborn?"

"Gaucho's right," Ben said. "Pop won't let us."

"Señor Pop is right," Gaucho said. "He is big man."

"Yes," Ben agreed. "Pop's all right."

"But King was a slick—till we branded him," Dixie said. "Under the range law, that makes him ours."

"Yes, but Pop doesn't always hold to the letter of the law," Ben said.

"Not if it's on the other fellow's side," Dixie said.

"Is good big man," Gaucho said, admiration in his voice.

"If it's Mr. Blair's horse, it's Mr. Blair's horse, as far as Pop is concerned," Ben said.

"Well, is it?" Dixie demanded bluntly. "Is King Mr. Blair's colt?"

Ben hesitated a long time before answering, then said, "Yes, I think he is." He had to be honest with Dixie and the gaucho.

Ben's admission was followed by a dismal silence, then Dixie said, "Well, what're we going to do? What can we do? It would make me sick to see King leave the high country."

"Me, too," Ben said. "Maybe we can think of something. I'll try."

CHAPTER FOUR

B EN TRIED. He lay awake on his bed in the big loft bunk
room most of the night trying to think of some way
they could save King, could keep him in the high country
to lead his band of mares and sire good colts. But when
Vince's call, "Breakfast, boys," came booming up the stairs,
Ben had to admit that he was as far from a solution as ever.

This was one morning when Ben did not want to get up.
Even the rich warm smells of breakfast coming from the
kitchen failed to enthuse him. He heard the springs on
Steve's bed squeak, heard Steve yawn, and later get into his
levis and stamp on his boots. Steve crossed the floor and
thumped down the stairs.

A hand fell on Ben's shoulder and shook him gently.
"Time for get up, Ben," the gaucho's voice said. "Breakfast, she is ready."

"Okay, I'm awake," Ben said.

He waited until he heard the gaucho go down before he
got out of bed. He wasn't happy this morning. When presently he reached the kitchen, the others were around the

big table, already eating. He pulled back his chair and sat down.

Vince, at the head of the table, looked up and said, "Have you washed yet?"

Ben got up and went out on the porch, doused his hands and face with the cold, clear water, wet his yellow hair and combed it, feeling that everything was wrong with this morning. Yesterday, out of school and back helping with the work on the ranch, he had been happy and carefree. Today everything was spoiled.

Back in the kitchen, Dixie gave him a quizzical look. Ben ignored it. There was nothing he could do, nothing that could be done. Dixie might just as well forget the whole matter. He might as well, too. In fact, he decided that he would. He would forget all about the wild horses up in Twin Buttes; he would even stop riding up there. He didn't want to watch them, not with King gone. In a few years they would go back to being broomtails and scrubs.

But Dixie did not intend to forget it. "What about King, Pop?" she said presently.

"What about what?" Vince said gruffly. It was a subject that all of them had been avoiding.

"King," Dixie said. "What're we going to do about him?"

"What is there for us to do about him?" Vince said, cutting a square of thick ham.

"Mr. Blair will be back today," Dixie said. "Are you going to let him take King?"

Vince's face looked as though he had not slept much either. "Well," he said, "if he's Mr. Blair's horse, that's all there is to it. There's nothing for us to do. It's up to Mr. Blair."

"He's got our brand on him," Dixie said. "That should give us some kind of a claim on him."

"Not if he's a stolen horse," Vince said.

"But how were we to know it?" Dixie said. "He was a slick, running with a wild bunch."

"No way," Vince said. "I don't blame you and Ben. There wasn't any way you could tell he was stolen."

Dixie tossed her head and said, "It's not fair. We looked after him, we branded him, we kept Tom Sample from getting him."

"The wild bunch needs him up there, Pop," Ben said. "It needs him bad."

"That's not the point," Vince said severely. "The point is who his real owner is. We've got to think about the other person's rights."

"As I see it," Dixie said, "the wild horses have rights too. But nobody pays any attention to them." She was annoyed and did not bother to disguise it.

Vince turned a reproving eye on her and said, "Horses are not people, Dixie."

"If they were, they wouldn't stand for the way they're treated sometimes," the girl said.

"Dixie, get the rest of the ham from the stove," her mother said, realizing that the argument was not going to produce any desirable results. Dixie's tongue seemed unusually sharp this morning and Vince's temper was unusually testy.

With the black stallion thus banned as a subject of conversation, everyone found that he had nothing to say, and the breakfast was finished in a strained and somewhat unhappy silence. Ben was finished first. "Excuse me," he said, and got up and went out the back door, taking his hat from its nail on the porch. He decided that he was washing his hands of the whole matter; his father could handle it as he wished.

Ben went to the barn and saddled Inky. The others—Vince, Steve and the gaucho—were coming from the house as Ben rode away. He went down the creek. There were some cows up in Wolf Creek Canyon that should be looked after. And Ben decided that today he would find Tanger. Tanger, a good chestnut gelding by Keister, was Ben's other horse. Dixie had ridden him to the little grade school, four miles away, during the winter and had turned him out several weeks before when the school closed for the summer. Now Ben, foreseeing a summer of riding, wanted to bring the chestnut in as a relief for Inky. Of course there were other horses that he could ride if the need arose, but Tanger, like Inky, was his own, and had a warm place in his affections.

But despite his decision at the breakfast table, Ben found that it was not easy to get his thoughts away from the black stallion. Old Three Deck Ridge lay to his left as he rode, and at the head of Three Deck lay Bascomb Flats and Lake

Basin and Gailey Ridge and all the wide rugged Twin Buttes country where, at this season of the year, the wild horses roamed. Ever since he had returned from Boise, Ben had planned that, at the first opportunity, he would ride up there and have a look at old King. Each spring he was always anxious to find out how the wild horses had wintered down in the Owyhee breaks, where they were driven by the snow. A few, usually the old ones whose teeth were bad and who became weak on the coarse winter food, failed to return, due to starvation or the cougars and wolves that followed them into the rough canyons. King, of course, was still a powerful horse and there was little likelihood of his falling prey to the cougars. But there were other possibilities, such as falls and broken legs, and Ben always felt relieved when he knew that King was back on the summer range and in good condition. So he had planned to go up there, but now he had little heart to go. What was the use of worrying about King any longer? He almost wished that something had happened, not that King had been killed, of course, but that something might have happened to keep him away from Twin Buttes that summer.

The cows and calves in Wolf Creek were in good shape. Ben saw some coyote sign but no injuries or any indication that the little wolves were numerous enough to bother the calves. A few Tack horses were running in there too, mostly mares and colts. Tanger, however, was not with them.

Up in the canyon, Ben turned his horse against the

Three Deck slope, found a faint trail, and held his elevation on the side of the ridge until presently he came around to its crest, at a point halfway between the first and second flats or "decks" that gave the ridge its name. The beaten trail on the crest led up to Twin Buttes, and Ben hesitated as he looked along it, before reining Inky downward.

After a time Ben came to a shoulder, from which he could see down into Crystal Canyon. He pulled his horse to a halt and sat in the saddle, looking down at the barns and corrals and the green fields which made up Tack, and he knew a pride and a pleasure in its well-kept condition and in its solid security.

A few minutes later, as Ben rode on down the trail, a lifting dust across Crystal Creek Canyon to the north caught his attention, and the discontentment of the morning returned. Ben looked down at the ranch again. The gaucho was working a colt in the little round corral near the barn, but there was no sign of Steve or his father.

Ben was nearing the creek when the long, heavy car came in sight along the rutted road that came down into the canyon from the west. He rode through the water and up to the breaking corral, pausing for a minute to watch the gaucho ease a saddle onto the back of a nervous colt. The colt was ready to fight and Ben knew it might be days before the gaucho would climb into his sheepskin-covered saddle. He went on, entered the barn runway, and halted behind Inky's stall. He took off the bridle and loosened the saddle cinch, to give the horse an opportunity to rest in the cool shadows during the noon period.

Leaving the barn by the door nearest the house, Ben saw that the big car had come to a halt in the yard. The two men had left it to escape the heat and were sitting on the edge of the porch in the shade. Ben had an impulse to turn back into the barn but they had already seen him.

"Hi, Ben," Tom Sample called.

Ben went along the path to them.

"Good morning, Ben," Andy Blair said, smiling in a friendly manner.

"Good morning," Ben said. "Have you seen Pop?"

"Not yet," Blair said. "We just arrived."

Dixie came from the house then; and, because she was wearing a dress, Ben knew she had not been riding. "Won't you come inside?" she said to Andy Blair. "Dinner'll be ready in about a half hour."

"Thanks," Blair said, "but we'll just wait out here. It's nice and cool. We want to see your father."

"He went up the canyon," Dixie said, "but he'll be back for dinner. He didn't know just when you'd get here."

"That's all right," Blair said. "We don't mind waiting. Do you go to school at that house we saw back along the road?"

"I do," she said, "but Ben goes to Boise. Next year I'll finish here and then I'll go to Boise too."

"I bet you'll like that," the man said.

"I think I will, but Ben doesn't," she said.

"Aw, Dix," Ben said.

"You'd rather be out here on the ranch, riding horses?" Blair said to Ben.

"Yes, sir," Ben said.

"But schooling is necessary these days," Blair said. "There'll be plenty of time afterward."

"I guess so," Ben said.

Tom Sample had another subject on his mind, and this small talk made him impatient. "What about the horse, Ben?" he said. "You're not going to claim he's not Mr. Blair's colt, are you?"

Ben had begun to feel friendly but now he froze again.

"Anybody that knows horses can look at the picture and tell it's the same animal," Tom Sample said.

"If you could have had your way, he wouldn't even be up there now," Dixie said pointedly.

"I'd have turned him over to Mr. Blair," Tom said.

Dixie snorted disbelievingly.

"I certainly hope that I am not going to cause you any sorrow," Andy Blair said. "I don't want to do that. I can understand how you feel about this black stallion, but . . . well, you can understand how I feel about Midnight Chief. For seven years, nearly eight now, I've been looking for him, hoping that I could get him back. You see, he's the only son Midnight Fire ever had. That makes him a pretty important horse."

"But you don't know that he's King," Dixie said.

"That's right, I don't," he answered.

"I do," Tom Sample said. "I'm sure of it."

"Tom is so certain, he gives me hope," Blair said. "But I would like to know what you and Ben think. From what I hear, you two have seen more of this black stallion than anyone else."

"We've been watching him up there for four years," Dixie said. "We caught him once, with the gaucho helping us."

The man nodded. "I heard about that. That was when you branded him. I don't censure you for branding him; I'd have probably done the same thing. And I know the range law. If it was any other horse, I'd just forget it. But I can't forget Midnight Chief. Do you think it's the same one?"

Dixie hesitated, then said, "I don't know. I saw the picture and I've seen King, but there are a lot of black horses that look alike."

"What about your father?" Blair said. "What does he say?"

"Pop has never seen King, not up close," she said.

"What do you say, Ben?" Tom Sample said. "What do you think about it?"

Ben resented Tom Sample's pushing at him with questions, but out of respect to Mr. Blair he felt obliged to answer and he said, "It could be."

"Could be?" Tom cried. "You know it is. You might just as well admit it."

"You plan to go up there after him anyway, don't you?" Dixie said, her eyes flashing.

Blair spoke then. "I'll not touch a horse with another man's brand on it unless I can prove beyond a doubt it is mine," he said. "But I believe your father is fair. I can't tell myself; I've never seen the stallion. I am depending on you Darbys to help me out in this thing."

"It's your horse, Mr. Blair," Tom Sample said. "I'd swear to that."

"Tom's swearing doesn't mean much around here," Dixie said to Mr. Blair, and seemed to enjoy the flare of temper in Sample's eyes.

Ben was struggling with conflicting emotions. He would have liked to tell Tom Sample to get off Tack and stay off, but he could not treat Mr. Blair like that. He had to be fair to Mr. Blair. Presently he said, "I don't know. It could be, I guess. But it seems to me that you can tell better than anyone else. Midnight Chief, if he is still alive, will probably look more like Midnight Fire than the colt did. You're the only one of us who has seen Midnight Fire."

"That's what I've been telling you, Mr. Blair," Tom Sample said. "We ought to go on up there and have a look. It's free country."

"I want to talk to Mr. Darby about it first," Blair said.

"It's all right," Ben said slowly. "It'll be all right. I guess I could take you up there."

"We won't need him," Tom Sample said. "I know that country. All we need is a couple of horses."

Mr. Blair was looking at Ben. "I'd like you to take us, if you will, Ben," he said. "I'd like you to be up there when I see the stallion."

"All right," Ben said. "I'll take you."

"I think I'll just go along too," Dixie said.

"We can start right away, right after we eat," Tom Sample said.

"If we do, you can expect to spend the night up there," Ben said. "It'll be a long day's ride to find them and get back here."

Blair looked at Tom with a puzzled expression. "I thought you said you knew that country?" he said.

"Oh, I figured to take bedrolls," Tom said. "I didn't see any need of wastin' half a day."

"We'll start in the morning," Mr. Blair said to Ben.

Vince Darby came pounding along the path from the barn on his high heels. He paused, and his keen eyes ran over the group. The gaucho was behind him. "Come on in," Vince said. "Come on in. Let's eat. We can talk about horses in there."

CHAPTER FIVE

THE SKY slowly flushed pink as they rode up old Three Deck Ridge. As they reached the top, where the ridge merges into Bascomb Flats, the sun broke suddenly from the horizon beyond Twin Buttes and spilled its early morning gold across the land.

Ben halted Inky by slightly flexing his wrist. "There's his country, Mr. Blair," Ben said. He knew that after the climb up the ridge, a few seconds of rest would do the horses good. So Ben sat there, watching the light play across the tips of the brush.

Andy Blair was riding a showy bay with white hind feet and a blaze in his face. The bay stopped beside Ben's horse and Andy Blair sat there silently.

Dixie rode behind Andy Blair, on the gaucho's sweet Listo mare, and Tom Sample brought up the rear, on another Keister colt.

When Tom's horse halted, he said, "He'll likely be at Basin Lake, Mr. Blair. That's where I nearly always find him. That's his favorite water hole."

Still gazing into the morning's fresh glory, Andy Blair did not answer.

"When were you up here last?" Dixie asked Tom, knowing full well that it had been two years.

Tom said, "I rode this country before you were born, my little lady."

Ben touched his horse on, headed for the broken nose of old Gailey Ridge which divided the view before them like a high rock-ribbed fin.

After they had ridden a mile or so, Tom Sample pushed his horse up and said, "We ought to head for Basin Lake. That's where they'll be. There's water there and good feed."

"Could be," Ben said, but without changing his course.

"You're wasting a lot of time," Tom said. "No wonder it takes you all day to get up here and find them."

"Maybe," Ben said.

"We'll find them," Dixie said. "If you want to go to Basin Lake, the way's open."

Tom dropped back, grumbling under his breath. Dixie hoped that he might leave them but knew that he would not. Tom was determined to be present when Andy Blair saw the black stallion.

Up on Gailey's Nose, Ben pulled to a halt. The rough, brushy country spread wide before them on both sides of the ridge.

"There they are," Tom Sample said suddenly, after a brief survey. He lifted his hand and pointed to the north.

"Where?" Andy Blair said.

"There—just to the right of that draw." Tom pushed his horse up close to Andy's and pointed again.

"There are some more over here," Dixie said, looking to the right, toward Standing Rock.

"I see them now," Andy Blair said, following Tom's pointing. "Or, at least, I see something, but I can't tell whether they're horses or cows."

"They're horses," Ben said, taking his binoculars out of their battered leather case. He had bought them in Nampa, with money from the sale of his orphaned steer, just to use in watching the wild horses.

"There they are," Ben said presently.

"They're headed for Basin Lake, just like I said," Tom Sample said.

"Yes," Ben said, handing the glasses to Andy Blair.

Blair looked through the glasses a long time, then said, "They are a long distance away, but I don't see any black stallion. At least, I can't pick him out."

"I didn't see him either," Ben said.

"Maybe you've got the wrong horses," Tom said.

When Andy Blair had finished with the glasses, Ben handed them to Dixie and said, "What do you think?"

She took her time, then nodded.

Tom Sample had been impatient for the glasses, and now Ben handed them to him. Tom dismounted and steadied his elbows on a rock. He looked for a long time, then turned and said, "He's not there, Mr. Blair. He's not with that bunch."

"You sure?"

"Yes. There's three or four dark horses, but they're not him."

Andy Blair turned questioning eyes to Ben.

"He's down there," Ben said. "That's his bunch. We can get a good look at them at Basin Lake. They'll water there a little before sundown."

Tom Sample had turned his glasses in the direction of Standing Rock and presently he said, "There! I see him! There he is, with that bunch over there. See that black, on the far side? That's him, Mr. Blair. That's your colt."

"Where? Where?" Andy Blair asked, a note of excitement coming into his voice. His hands trembled as he took the glasses.

"There. The far horse," Tom Sample said, pointing.

Blair looked, then got down and found a rock on which to steady the glasses.

Dixie looked at Ben, and Ben shrugged but said nothing.

"I knew I could find him," Tom said triumphantly.

Andy Blair put the glasses down. "It's too far to tell," he said. "It's too far to tell much about him."

"We'll go down," Tom said. "We'll ride down there. I can get you close to him."

Andy Blair looked at Ben.

Ben nodded. "We can get pretty close to them, I think. Close enough."

Blair mounted his horse and said, "Let's go down."

Tom Sample pushed up to the front. "I've got it all figured out," he said, as they turned their horses down the south slope. "We'll head off to the west and keep behind that rise. Then we can get in that gully and follow **it**. That'll bring us up on their down-wind side. These **wild** horses can smell like mule deer, Mr. Blair."

Blair nodded and followed Tom.

"If you ask me, they smell like horses," Dixie said dryly.

"You know what I mean," Tom said sharply.

Ben held Inky back, letting Tom Sample have the lead, and Dixie rode behind Ben. All morning long she had been staying between Tom and Andy Blair, so that whenever Tom wanted to speak to Blair he had to talk around her or over her head, but now she let them ride together, and Tom was very confident of himself.

They made the long, careful approach under Tom's direction and two hours later reached a place in the gully where Tom pulled his horse to a halt. "They're right out there," Tom said in a low voice. "We'll leave our horses here and crawl up to the edge on our bellies."

"Here," Ben said, extending the glasses to Andy Blair.

"Ssssh, not so loud," Tom said.

"All right," Ben said, lowering his voice.

They dismounted, and Tom and Andy Blair crawled up the side of the gully to its lip. Here they cautiously raised themselves, to look over the brush. Then, after a few seconds, Tom stood up and looked around with a puzzled expression on his face.

"What's the matter?" Ben asked.

"They're not here," Andy Blair said. "They're gone. There's not a horse in sight."

"They smelled us," Tom Sample said. "The wind must

have changed, while we were coming along the draw."

Ben climbed up and looked around. "They were feeding east," he said. "There's good grass beyond that nose. I wouldn't be surprised if they're over there."

Tom Sample considered a second, then said, "Sure, that's where they are. They were working in that direction." He slid back into the gully and mounted his horse.

With Tom leading, they rode to the nose and presently reached its crest. Tom stood in his stirrups, peering over. Suddenly he ducked down and motioned them to be silent with his hand. "Here they are," he said in a loud whisper.

Andy Blair dismounted and went forward eagerly, still clutching the binoculars. Ben and Dixie followed more slowly. The horses were feeding, well out in the brush. Ben counted nine of them, besides the black stallion, which was feeding alone, beyond the general scattering.

"There he is, Mr. Blair," Tom Sample said. "That's the horse we've been looking for." His voice was low but confident.

Andy Blair had the binoculars to his eyes. He looked for a long time, then crept up farther, where he could kneel and rest his elbows on a clump of brush. He twisted the focus ring.

"See him, beyond the others?" Tom Sample said.

Ben looked at Dixie, and Dixie looked back at him. There were odd wrinkles around her clear blue eyes as if she were somehow perplexed.

Presently Andy Blair turned around and sat on the ground, facing them. His eyes were dull and the binoculars hung loosely from the fingers of his left hand. "It's not the one," he said, his voice croaking with disappointment.

"But . . . but, Mr. Blair . . ." Tom Sample said. "That's the black stallion."

"It's not Midnight Fire's son," Blair said positively.

"But . . . you can't see him good, not from here," Tom said desperately. "We'll get closer to him, so you can really see him."

Blair stood up, indifferent now to the effect his action would have on the feeding horses. "I've seen all I need to," he said with a weary voice. "I've been afraid all along this was the way it would be, Tom. It was too good to be true."

"But . . . but . . ." Tom said, helplessly.

"Let's get back to the ranch," Andy Blair said.

Out in the brush the wild horses, having become aware of the men, started to move away. The challenging whinny of the stallion came to their ears faintly, but none of them even bothered to look. Andy Blair handed the binoculars to Ben and mounted the bay. He turned the animal and headed through the sage, in the direction of Gailey's Nose. Tom Sample rode after him, crushed and stunned.

Dixie looked at Ben, and Ben looked back at her. "Come on," Ben said roughly.

The sun poured its midday heat down into the brush, and the horse's feet brought up a fine dust that hung suspended in the air. Occasionally one of the horses blew its nose, with a long fluttering sound.

Andy Blair rode in front, silent and disappointed. Tom Sample rode behind Blair, now and then shaking his head, as if he could not understand what had happened. Dixie and Ben let their horses fall back, until they were some distance from the others.

"We've got a lunch," Dixie said presently, letting her hand drop to the bundle tied behind her saddle. Milly had prepared it for them that morning while they ate breakfast.

"I guess Mr. Blair isn't hungry," Ben said.

"It's got chocolate cookies in it," she said.

Ben called them. "Tom, are you and Mr. Blair hungry?"

Neither of them paid any attention to him.

"We could eat the cookies," Dixie said.

"I'll take one," Ben answered.

She untied the bundle and unwrapped it without halting her horse. She got a handful of cookies and Ben took several of them. Later they had a drink from Ben's canteen.

The two men in front rode on steadily, paying no attention to the boy and girl following them.

Dixie and Ben became lost in their thoughts too. After a time, Dixie looked at Ben and said, "What're you going to do about it?"

"About what?" Ben said sharply.

"You know what I'm talking about," she said.

Ben's eyes turned down to his horse's ears. "Nothing," he said after a few seconds.

Dixie was silent and Ben let the matter rest there while they rode a quarter of a mile. "Why should I do anything?" he said. "I didn't have anything to do with it."

"No," she said. "It's not your fault." This was followed

by another long silence, then she said, "How much did Mr. Blair give you?"

"Twenty dollars," Ben said. "Pop wouldn't take anything for the use of the horses, so Mr. Blair gave me twenty dollars . . . to bring him up here."

"To show him the black stallion," Dixie said. "That's what he paid you for."

"Well?" Ben said angrily.

"It doesn't seem exactly fair."

Ben didn't reply for several minutes, then he blurted, "I'll give him his old twenty dollars back. I didn't want to take it anyway. I was going to give you half of it."

She shook her head. "I don't believe I want any of it."

"Darn it, Dixie," Ben said, "I haven't done anything."

"No," she said. "No, you haven't. I don't believe Mr. Blair will take the money back. He's not that kind."

"Yes, he will."

"No, he won't, not unless—"

"Unless what?"

"Unless you tell him why."

"Darn it, Dix, you know I can't do that!"

"Yes, I know you can't."

"Well—?"

"Well?"

Ben lapsed into an uncomfortable silence. He leaned forward and smoothed the mane on Inky's neck. "Tom Sample did it," he said. "It's not my fault."

"But that's what he hired you for."

"Gee whiz," Ben said. "I wish I hadn't brought him up here. Do you know what this might do, Dix . . . what it might mean?"

"Yes, but it wouldn't have made any difference if we hadn't come. Tom would have taken him to Basin Lake."

"Yes," Ben said, but the knowledge did little to relieve his gloom.

"You know what Pop will think about it," she said.

"Do we have to tell him? Can't you keep anything to yourself? Gee whiz!"

"Sure," she said. "I don't have to tell him; I didn't get the twenty dollars. And I won't take any part of it."

Ben considered the matter several minutes longer, then he raised his head and looked around. Gailey's rugged nose was to their right. "Okay," he said, "okay. Now you stay out of this and keep your mouth shut."

He increased Inky's gait to a trot. Dixie followed close behind him.

"These horses need water," he said, catching up with the two men in front. "We'd better swing by Basin Lake."

Andy Blair blinked his eyes, as if just waking up, and looked down at his horse's shoulders for signs of sweat. Tom Sample said, "Heck, Ben, that's six or seven miles out of the way."

Andy Blair said, "They don't seem very hot, Ben. We haven't been riding hard."

"They ought to have a drink," Ben insisted.

"It's not more than fifteen miles to the ranch," Tom Sample said. "We'll be there before dark."

"We should have gone into Juniper Springs," Dixie said. "We always water our horses when we come up here on a hot day like this."

"It's silly," Tom said. "I won't do it. I'm not going to ride ten miles out of the way to water a horse that don't need it."

"They're Tack horses and I say they need water," Ben said flatly. "If you don't like it, Tom, you can get off and walk."

"Yeah," Tom growled. "Wait till Vince hears about this."

Andy Blair blinked his eyes some more and said, "Of course, Ben, if you think we should. I'm in something of a hurry to get back, but if you say we should . . ."

"Come on," Ben said, turning Inky to the northeast.

Dixie and Mr. Blair followed him immediately but Tom Sample hesitated awhile, grumbling to himself, then kicked his horse into an angry gallop after them. Catching up, he jerked the horse to a dirt-raising stop.

"Tack horses are not used to that kind of treatment," Ben said to him quietly.

"When I'm riding them, they do like I want them to," Tom answered shortly.

Andy Blair eyed Tom sharply.

Dixie said, "I wish he'd buck you off."

"He can try, any time he's ready," Tom said boastfully.

Ben turned his face back to the front and kept Inky stepping freely. He watched the horizon, and after an hour or so he saw the tops of the trees clustered on the east bank of Basin Lake. Ben's keen eyes could detect a haze of dust

[63]

against the green and he angled slightly more to the left.

"Where're you going now?" Tom Sample said. "Basin Lake's over there."

"I'll get there," Ben replied and kept riding.

Presently they were in shoulder-high brush and there was no trail through it. Ben wove his horse in and out and Dixie left her place between the two men and pushed up abreast of him. "Keep quiet," Ben growled at her.

A little farther on, Inky raised his head, put his short ears foward and, of his own accord, came to a halt. Listo halted also.

"Why, there's horses here," Tom Sample said, coming up behind them.

"Yes," Ben said.

A band of horses—bays, blacks, sorrels and grays—were scattered over the grass near the lake grazing.

Andy Blair came up beside Ben. His horse halted. "What's this?" he said. "What horses are these?"

Just then the stallion sighted them. He flung up his head, stood like a statue for an instant, then sent forth his shrill challenging neigh. The mares and colts became instantly alert. The stallion came toward the riders, lifting his knees in high belligerent action.

Ben turned so he could see Andy Blair's face. The man was pale and his eyes fairly bulged out of his head. His mouth was half open and he seemed powerless to close it. His hand reached out and caught Ben's arm, and his fingers closed tightly as if to keep him from falling. When finally he spoke his voice was hardly more than a whisper, "Fire

. . . Midnight Fire . . ." Then Ben looked away, because there were tears rolling down the man's cheeks.

"That's him," Tom Sample cried excitedly. "That's him, Mr. Blair. That's the horse I've been telling you about. See him!"

Ben had hoped against this, had hoped that a casual sighting of the black stallion would bring no recollection to Andy Blair. Now he knew he had lost. In addition to his own sadness, he somehow felt that he had betrayed a friend who trusted him. He and Dixie—and the gaucho—were the only people who knew the black stallion, who understood him.

Knowing full well what it all meant, Dixie was downcast too, but she used the opportunity for a sarcastic dig at Tom Sample. "You sure, Tom?" she said. "He certainly did get over here in a hurry."

The wild horses were going away now, with King circling watchfully behind them.

"I'd know him in a thousand," Andy Blair said. "I never could mistake that head."

"I told you," Tom said. "I knew it was him. When I saw that picture of Midnight Fire, I knew this was his colt. I told you."

"I can't believe it," Blair said, "not after all these years. He's Midnight Fire all over again. Let's get closer to them."

The horses were well out in the brush now, still going away.

"We can't get any closer, not today," Ben said. "It's time we headed back to the ranch."

They were halfway back to the head of Three Deck when Dixie, catching Ben's eye, pointed to the canteen tied to Ben's saddle. At first Ben thought she wanted a drink and then he realized that they had not watered their horses at Basin Lake. But both Andy Blair and Tom Sample had been too excited to notice.

CHAPTER SIX

WILL HE be difficult to catch?" Andy Blair asked.
The narrowness of the Three Deck trail forced them to ride in single file. Ben was in front and Andy Blair rode behind him. Dixie, as usual, had edged herself between Blair and Tom Sample, and the Arizona man turned in his saddle to ask the question over Dixie's felt hat. In their elation over the certainty that the black stallion was actually Midnight Fire's colt, the two men seemed to have forgot Ben and Dixie. Now Ben, without looking back, felt a tightening of interest at Blair's question.

"Not for me, he won't," Tom said with breezy confidence. "You see I know these wild horses; I've been running them for years. I've caught hundreds of them."

"You didn't get him two years ago," Dixie said.

"I would have," Tom said in a quick reply. "I had him run down. That's the only reason Ben ever got his hands on him to put on that brand. I had him in a trap once before that."

"But he didn't stay," Dixie said. "And he wasn't run down, not by any means."

"How long will it take?" Mr. Blair said.

"Well, that's a little hard to say," Tom said. "The bunch is pretty wild and you can see they're in good shape. They're going to cover some country before they're ready to quit. I'd figure about two weeks."

"That long?"

"That's after we get set up," Tom went on to explain. "I'll bring my crew up and we'll camp at Basin Lake and work from there. That's one of his regular water holes."

"But I'm in a hurry; I want to get back home," Mr. Blair said.

"You can't hurry catching wild horses," Tom said. "It'll take a lot of hard riding. I've got a bunch of good men and we'll grain our saddle horses, but still it'll take some time."

"Is all that necessary?" Mr. Blair said. "Will he be that hard to catch?"

"Ask Ben," Tom said. "He knows."

"What about it, Ben?" Mr. Blair said.

"He'll be hard to catch," Ben said briefly, still not looking around.

"Of course," Tom said, "if I can get him in a trap, it won't take so long. I know where there's a good trap in a canyon, with the fences already built. It won't take long to put it in shape."

"You won't get him in there—not again," Dixie said.

"How do you know I won't?" Tom said, irritation coming into his voice. "What do you know about wild horses? Did you ever catch any?"

"One," she said. "The one you're after. I helped do it."

Tom had no ready reply to that.

Andy Blair said, "How soon can you start?"

"As soon as we get back to town," Tom said. "Of course, it will take a few days to get the boys together and get everything ready. We will have to bring a lot of horses in, four or five for each man. And they have to be good. You don't catch wild horses on old plugs. We'll relay them and keep them away from the water holes. Four or five days without water slows them down plenty."

Up in front, Ben nodded to himself. Sure, that was the way Tom would catch King; that was the standard pattern. Run them till they were so weary and sore footed they couldn't run any more. It was rough on the horses; the suckling colts would drop out, and some of the old animals would be so weak they would die during the winter. But who cared about that? Who cared so long as they got the horse they wanted? Just then Ben began to feel an aversion to Andy Blair. He seemed like a nice man, but he was going to be part of all that was to happen in the high country during the next few weeks.

"All I want is Midnight Chief," Blair said.

"Sure, I know," Tom said. "But while we're at it, we might as well make a sweep. It won't take any more time or work. I'm in the horse business and there are some young horses up there I can use, if you don't want them. We might as well take the best ones while we're at it."

"Yes, I guess so," Andy Blair said. "I hadn't thought about that, but I guess we might as well. No one else owns them, I suppose?"

"Naw, they're just mustangs. The country'll be better off without them."

Ben was too depressed to argue, but Dixie's strong little spirit was still unflagging. "It will not," she declared. "They're not hurting anything or anybody up there. It's the only place they've got left to live."

"You know better than that," Tom told her. "All the stockmen in this country would like to see them gone," he went on to Andy Blair. "Why, not so many years ago, they used to carry rifles and shoot them on sight."

This, Dixie knew, was generally true. There had been so many wild horses when the cattlemen first came that it was a common practice to kill them to conserve the range for cattle. They had been driven into the back country and their numbers had become so few that in recent years the ranchers had paid little attention to them. But the old prejudice still survived and most of the stockmen, as Tom said, believed that the country would be better without them. Even her father shared this opinion, but she knew that, despite his gruffness and lack of regard for wild horses in general, there was a warm place in his heart for all horses.

"All right," Andy Blair agreed.

"Sure," Tom said. "We'll take the whole bunch. The ranchers in this country will thank you for it. I'll take them as part of my pay. That way it won't cost you as much to get Midnight Chief. It is a good deal for everybody."

"Except the horses," Dixie said.

Ben turned his head. "Shut up, Dix," he said, not angrily. There was no use in arguing any more. All this was inevitable. Of course, Tom would take advantage of the opportunity to catch as many horses as he could. Tom had always wanted the wild horses. The ones that were worth anything would be traded and sold to riders, and the rest would be shipped to the canners at so much a pound. Tom Sample would get a profit on everything.

"Of course, the mustangs aren't worth much," Tom said to Andy Blair. "I might get a saddle horse or two out of the bunch, but most of them will go for chicken feed."

Tom was already, Ben reflected, trying to beat Mr. Blair down on the value of the wild horses. But they would be worth a great deal when Tom had them finally in his possession and was offering them for sale. Ben was unable to resist saying, "I'll give you a hundred dollars for the pick of the bunch, Tom."

Tom Sample laughed. "Smart boy," he said to Andy Blair. "Yes sir, Ben's a pretty clever fellow." But from the tone in his voice Ben knew that Tom didn't mean the compliment, that Tom was just laughing off the question he had raised about the value of the horses. "I wouldn't take your money, Ben," he went on, "but if there's any horses that look like they might make saddle stock, I'll give you one."

Andy Blair nodded his head in approval of this, but Ben had no faith in Tom Sample. Tom, he was sure, didn't mean it. And he felt that he had been drawn into a false position, for the offer seemed to clinch Tom's contention that the horses would be of little value.

"There'll be some Midnight Chief colts," Andy Blair said. "Some of his colts will be in the bunch."

"But out of broomtail mares," Tom said. "You don't get much out of a broomtail mare."

"No, I suppose not," Blair said.

Ben had an impulse to speak. There were some good mares up there; he knew because he had seen them. But he said nothing. To a man like Andy Blair, who set such great store on pedigrees, probably any horse in a wild bunch would be considered a broomtail. Andy Blair would think merely that Ben didn't know what he was talking about. Ben knew that with King gone there would be a difference in the band; King was the force that kept the wild band alive and vital and good. After King was gone some other stallion would take over, perhaps one of the scrawny inbred runts or an old pan-footed bay.

Ben pushed his horse down the ridge and across Crystal Creek. Gaucho's colts were in the breaking corral and the sheepskin saddle was on a rail, so Ben knew that the rider had finished his day's work and had gone to the house. Ben led the way around the barn to the gate of the main horse corral and dismounted. Without a word he started stripping off his saddle. The others halted in the gathering dusk.

Vince Darby came along the path from the house. "Supper's ready," he said. "Did you have a good trip?"

"We found him," Andy Blair said. "We found Midnight Fire's colt, Mr. Darby. The minute I saw him I knew it. He's got old Midnight Fire's head."

"You're sure of it?" Vince said.

"I couldn't be mistaken. If you had ever seen Midnight Fire, you would know I couldn't."

Vince was silent a second or two, then said, "Come on to the house. It's time to eat."

"I'll take care of your horse, Mr. Blair," Ben said, taking the animal's reins.

Tom Sample went with them, leaving his horse for Ben and Dixie to look after. Dixie made a grimace behind his back and said, "Somehow I just can't like him."

"I guess he doesn't care," Ben said, taking off his saddle. "He knows we can't stop him now."

Dixie pulled off her saddle and took Listo into the dark barn runway. She came back and said, "I wish we could. I wish there were something we could do."

"I do too," Ben said. He unsaddled the horse Mr. Blair had ridden and turned it into the corral, where there was hay in the rack.

"Can't you think of something?" Dixie said.

"No," Ben said.

"Try," Dixie said, irritation creeping into her voice.

"What do you think I've been doing?" Ben said. "There isn't anything—not anything Pop would stand for."

The gaucho came along the path from the house. "Supper, she is ready," he said. "Listo give you a good ride, no?"

"She's fine," Dixie said. "I put her in a stall for some grain."

Gaucho took the bridle off the horse Tom Sample had ridden. "The black stallion, she is el Señor Blair's?" he said.

"Yes," Ben said. There was no longer any question of it.

"Hola, what is?" Gaucho said, looking at the bit of the bridle he held. "Blood?" The bit had a red stain on it.

Ben and Dixie looked at the bit, and Ben nodded his head and said, "Tom cut his mouth when he jerked him up. Remember, Dixie?"

"El Señor Sample?" Gaucho asked.

"Yes. He was mad about something."

Gaucho shook his head.

"I'm going to tell Pop," Dixie said.

"No," Ben said. "It wouldn't do any good."

The gaucho slipped his hand into the horse's mouth and felt the jaw tissues behind the teeth. "Is only a little," he said presently. "El Señor Sample have—how you say it?— rough hand."

"I don't like him," Dixie said flatly.

"Come on," Ben said. "I'm hungry."

Milly had set extra plates at the big table for Andy Blair and Tom Sample. There were hot biscuits and steak and mashed potatoes and cream gravy and fresh green beans from the garden.

But Andy Blair was almost too excited to eat. "I can hardly believe it yet, Mr. Darby," he said. "To tell you the truth, I had just about given up hope when I ran into Tom in Caldwell. It was a lucky thing for me that Tom had seen this stallion."

"I knew him the minute I saw the picture of Midnight Fire," Tom said modestly. "I told Mr. Blair I knew where his horse was."

"I still didn't believe it," Blair said. "I couldn't believe it—not until I saw him with my own eyes. It didn't seem possible that he could have been running with wild horses all these years."

"No, I guess not," Vince said, casting a side glance at Ben, who was giving his attention to his food.

"I'm going to take him back to Arizona," Andy Blair said. "You'll be hearing from him one of these days. His colts will be winning races all over the country."

"He might be a little hard to catch," Vince said.

"Oh, I'll take care of that," Tom Sample said.

"Yes," Andy said, "Tom's going to catch him for me. He has the men and the horses to do it."

Vince nodded and said, "I figured he would."

"It'll take a couple of weeks," Andy said, with some disappointment. "I'm in something of a hurry; I want to get back home because I have a yearling sale coming up. But Tom says it will take a couple of weeks."

"Yes, I expect it will," Vince said.

"He'll be lucky to do it in that time," Steve said. "I saw that stallion when we were up catching Ben's Christmas colt, and he won't be easy to run down."

"I'll get him," Tom said. "I've got some ideas."

Ben glanced up then, wondering what might be in

Tom's mind, and saw a confident smirk on the man's face.

"You'll need them," Steve said, "and a lot of good grain-fed horses, too."

Mr. Blair said, "I don't know a thing about wild horses. I'm leaving it all up to Tom."

"Vince knows I've caught lots of wild horses," Tom said.

"Yes," Vince said. "You'll be staying here tonight?" he went on to Andy Blair.

Andy shook his head. "We'll get back to town, so Tom can start getting things ready. But I want to thank you for all your kindness and assistance. I want to pay you for your trouble too. I know that you've been keeping your eye on Midnight Chief for years. You even put your brand on him to protect him. And you had a claim to him but you've been fair enough not to press it. I appreciate all that and I want to pay you for your trouble. What would you consider a fair amount?"

Vince considered the question a few minutes, then said, "I guess you should talk to Ben about that. He's the one who has been interested in King—he and Dixie."

"That's right," Andy Blair said. "What do you say, Ben —you and Dixie? How much do you want for King? I'm willing to pay any reasonable amount."

Ben looked at Dixie and Dixie looked at Ben.

"Come on," the man said, smiling at them. "Speak up. Don't be bashful. What would you say is right? What's a good horse worth in this country?"

Ben shook his head. "No," he said.

"No," Dixie said.

"But . . . I want to pay you," Andy Blair said. "It's worth it to me. I'll give you enough to buy another horse—even another good stallion."

"No," Ben said.

Dixie looked up at Andy Blair and said seriously, "We can't take anything—not for looking after King. You see . . . you see . . ." She didn't finish but pushed back her chair and got up and left the room.

Andy Blair's face took on a flustered look. "But I want to pay," he said to Vince Darby. " I want to pay you, man. How much do you want?" He reached into his pocket for his purse.

"No," Vince said. "No, you can't pay me either. I don't own King and if I did, I reckon I wouldn't sell him."

Ben could hardly see his plate for the mist in his eyes, but he heard his father's voice and he was proud of what his father had said. He knew that his father understood.

CHAPTER SEVEN

DESPITE Andy Blair's haste, it was four days before Tom Sample and his riders came back by Tack on their way to the high country. They crossed Crystal Canyon north of the ranch but Ben saw them. There were four riders and twenty-two horses, and half of the horses carried packs. Tom, Ben reflected grimly, was coming prepared.

Ben's glasses showed him that the leader was Tom himself, and the second man was Pearly Maunderland, the surly ex–bronc-rider. Maunderland, who fancied himself a horseman, was even more brutal than Tom. He was one man Vince Darby would not tolerate on Tack. This was the reason, Ben knew, that Tom was avoiding the ranch. At that distance, Ben did not recognize the other two riders, but assumed they were men of the same stamp. He watched while they climbed up out of the canyon and swung south.

Ben had known these riders were coming, but their actual appearance depressed him more than he had expected. He then felt that the last hope for King was gone. These men were shrewd, determined horse-runners and they would get him. King would give them a run and a fight, but in the end they would get him. Then Andy Blair would tie him in a trailer and head for Arizona, and that would be the last the Twin Buttes country would ever see of him. And King would not like being in Arizona; Ben was somehow sure of that. King would not be happy unless he were free, free to roam and run and challenge all the other horses that came within his vision. But these men cared nothing about that.

Arriving back at the ranch, Ben found that Andy Blair was there. Andy had left Tom's outfit and had come to Tack. Now he was at the corrals, talking to Vince. "Hello, Ben," he said, as Ben rode up.

"Hello," Ben answered and swung down.

"I'm on my way up to Twin Buttes," Blair said. "Tom and his men crossed above here."

Ben nodded. "I saw them. They swung over to Three Deck. You'll find their tracks up above the rim."

"I guess Tom plans to relay them?" Vince asked.

"He's got enough horses," Ben said.

"We're going to try to trap him first," Andy Blair said. "I want to get him as soon as possible. It took Tom longer to get ready than we thought it would."

"Trapping is best—if you can do it," Vince said.

"That's what I thought. It won't wear the horses down so much. Tom knows a place."

Ben knew the place too. It was a steep-walled little canyon that necked down in two places where pole fences could be built. Tom had trapped King and his band in there once, but the horses had broken down the fence. If King was as smart as Ben believed he was, he would not go in there again. But Ben saw no reason for giving them any advice.

"When we get him, I'd like to bring him down here," Andy Blair said. "This is the closest place to load him in a trailer."

Ben suddenly wished that his father would say no, that his father would say that it was up to Tom Sample to load the horse as well as catch him, but Vince, after a slight hesitation, said, "You can bring him here. That will be all right."

"Thanks," Andy Blair said heartily. "It'll save me time. Well, I guess I'd better be getting along. We'll be camped at Basin Lake. If you're up that way, drop in and see us. We brought in plenty of food."

Vince acknowledged the invitation with a nod of his head, but said, "I don't guess we'll be up that way."

"I'd be glad to have you, any time," Blair said. He swung up on his horse and rode away, taking the trail to the creek.

"I won't be going up that way," Ben said.

"I didn't figure you would," his father said. "Is Pearly Maunderland with Tom?"

"Yes, sir."

"Who else?"

"Two more men. I didn't know them. They had a big string of saddle horses."

Vince glanced down at his big hands and, after a few seconds, said, "I wish I could help you in this, son, but I don't know how. What's right is right, but sometimes the law seems to be pretty much out of joint, especially where horses are concerned."

Ben nodded miserably and said, "I know, Pop."

"I guess we ought not to think too much of them," Vince went on. "But a man's life would certainly be empty without a few good horses around."

"It's all right, Pop," Ben said. "It's just . . . I just hate to see him go. There's not another horse to take his place—not up there."

"There never is," Vince said. "Other horses come along, but the good ones always leave empty places. You always lose them, but having them is worth it."

Yes, having them was worth it, but during the next two or three days Ben hated to think about what was happening up in the high country. He could envision the wild bunch running through the brush with a horseman in pursuit, first one horseman and then another, each cunningly stationed at various points to keep the band moving. He could see the horses growing weary and becoming sore footed; he could see the exhausted colts dropping out and the black stallion coming back to drive the mares on. Round and round in a big circle they would go, not wise enough to realize that this very fact made it possible for the runners to relay them with a constant succession of fresh mounts. And in the end the colts and the old mares would be scattered over the country and the others would be so sore footed and weary that they could run no longer. Then Tom Sample and his men would move in with their ropes or force the band into a trap. And this time he couldn't help them; there wasn't a thing he could do.

But Ben was wrong about what was going on up in Twin Buttes, as he learned on the evening of the fourth day, when Andy Blair came riding down Three Deck trail. Andy pulled up at the corrals where Ben and Vince were unsaddling. There was a look of frustration on his face.

"Hello," Vince said.

"Hello, Mr. Darby. Hi, Ben." Blair swung down from his saddle, moving stiffly.

"Get hungry for a good meal?" Vince said.

"I'm hungry all right," the man said. "But that's not the reason I'm here. We're not making much progress up there."

"What's the matter? Can't you find any wild horses?" Vince said.

"We've found some wild horses, but they don't seem to be the right ones," Andy Blair said. "We've been up there four days now and haven't had a glimpse of Midnight Chief yet."

"No?" Vince said.

"That's a fact."

"Are you camped at Basin Lake?" Ben asked.

"Yes. We're camped right where we saw them the day you were up there with us."

"That's on his circle," Ben said. "He should be showing up there."

"That's what we figured, but he hasn't come. Two or three other bunches have come, and we ran one half a day before we discovered that it wasn't Midnight Chief. Say, those broomtails, as you call them, can really cover ground."

Ben grinned. Andy Blair was learning something about wild horses.

"What's happening," Vince surmised, "is that the stallion has winded you and he's been passing up Basin Lake. That's likely what he's doing."

"Well, he's certainly not coming in."

"You'll spot him eventually," Vince said. "Even in a country as big as that you'll find him, with five men riding."

"That's what Tom says," Blair said, "but I haven't any time to waste. I've got to get back home and get those yearlings ready for the sale."

Vince smiled and said, "It takes time to catch wild horses, there's no getting away from that."

"I don't want wild horses," Blair said. "I want just one horse."

"Well, it takes time to catch one, especially if he's the leader of the bunch," Vince said. "Usually the leader is the last one you get, if he's smart."

"And King is smart," Ben said.

"Well," said Andy Blair, "I don't know what to do, and I've got to do something."

"Pull the rigging off your horse and we'll go up and see what Milly has got for supper," Vince suggested. "I think she said something about gooseberry pie."

"I will," Blair said. "I'll stay overnight, if you can put

me up. But I wish you would tell me how I can get on the trail of that horse."

"I can't," Vince said. "It's too far away for me to know what's going on."

"Say," said Blair, "would you help me? Would you come up and get those fellows lined out? At the rate they're going now, it's going to take all summer to catch my horse."

Vince became serious and shook his head. "No, I don't think I can do that," he said. "I've got plenty to keep me busy here on the ranch."

Andy Blair was disappointed. Then he said, "What about Ben? Ben found him for us the other time. Would you let Ben come up and locate him for us? If he will just find him for us, we'll do the running. I'll pay him well."

Vince considered this and said, "How about it, Ben?"

"No," Ben said firmly.

"But you can find him, Ben. You know his range. You caught him once before."

"No," Ben repeated.

"But . . . I don't understand," Andy Blair said.

"I guess we've been beating around the bush a bit," Vince Darby said. "We'd like to help you, but you've got the wrong crew up there for us to work with."

"You mean Tom Sample?" Blair said.

"And Pearly Maunderland," Ben said. "I wouldn't help him catch wild horses, not for any amount of money."

"But why?" Blair said, in genuine bewilderment.

"We just don't think alike, not where horses are concerned," Vince said. "Anyhow, Tom wouldn't like us to move in. It would just be asking for trouble."

Blair said, "Then you won't help me?"

"About the only way we could do it," Vince said slowly, "would be for you to get rid of Tom Sample and his gang. If you'll do that, get them plumb out of there, then we might catch your horse for you. What would you think about that, Ben?" Vince was not certain that Ben would agree, even under those conditions.

Ben swallowed and said, "Yes." If King had to go, then he would rather help catch him than have Tom Sample do it. If he and Pop and the gaucho did it, they could save the young colts at least.

"But I can't do that," Andy Blair said. "I've got an agreement with Tom Sample. Of course, it's not written, but still I made a deal with him to catch Midnight Chief, if it turned out to be the colt."

"That being the case," Vince said, "there isn't anything we can do about it. Let's go wash up."

Andy Blair went back up Three Deck Ridge the next morning. Ben could not help feeling pleased at the lack of success which Tom Sample and his men were having, but he knew that it could not last. Tom and Pearly Maunderland would not be fooled very long. This was borne out a few days later when Andy Blair rode down the trail a second time.

Andy Blair was encouraged. "We've got them moving," he told Vince, "and we've got a couple of fences ready. It shouldn't take long now, but I can't wait any longer. I've got to get down to Arizona and get those yearlings sold. Just as soon as I can get away, I'll be back. I'd like to leave my horse here, if you could run me into town?"

"We'll do that, Andy," Vince said.

CHAPTER EIGHT

ANDY BLAIR left for Arizona, and for days after that no word came down from the high country. Nothing was seen at Tack of Tom Sample or any of his riders. They stayed far away from the Crystal Creek ranch.

It was haying season and the Darbys were busy in the fields. Ben and Steve rode the mowing machines and Vince did the raking. Acre after acre of the green alfalfa fell before the bright blades of the cutter bars and was gathered in long windrows to cure in the drying heat of the sun. Dixie helped her mother at the house. The gaucho, as usual, continued with his horse-breaking.

Ben did not care much for field work, but on a high-country ranch like Tack, hay was essential to carry the horses and cows through the winters, when the snow frequently lay deep and crusted on the slopes, so Ben rode the mower without complaint. Often however he glanced up at the Three Deck trail, half expecting to see Tom Sample and his men coming down with a big black stallion in tow. And Ben knew that the sight would sicken him.

The days passed however, one after another, and Tom Sample did not come down the ridge. Nor was anything heard of him or his riders. Ben thought that by now they surely would have been able to run down King. Of course he would put up a fight, but Tom and Pearly Maunderland knew how to handle horses, how to break them to their will. They would put ropes and halters and hobbles on him until he could hardly move. They would tie up his feet so he could not kick or rear or strike. They would starve him until he was weak, then yoke him between two heavy saddle horses. Oh, they would get him down that trail, Ben knew, even if they had to drag him.

But as the time passed Ben became more and more concerned. Evidently Tom and his men were having a difficult time, and Ben knew that meant a difficult time for King, too. Wherever the big horse was, he was in trouble. Maybe he was still moving wearily through the brush, trying to avoid the inevitable capture. Or perhaps he was already fighting against the ropes and the hobbles, against nooses that choked the strength from his big body. Ben tried to forget King, but he could not. His thoughts kept straying up to the high country, trying to help King fight his battles.

And presently, as day after day went by, another thought came to Ben. Suppose they did not bring King down to Tack? Tom Sample would be reluctant to come to the ranch without Andy Blair. Pearly Maunderland would be even still more reluctant, for his father had ordered him off the place once in no uncertain terms. In view of this, it was possible that they had decided to avoid the ranch and take their captives straight to town. They could easily have crossed the canyon above Tack without being seen. Ben realized, with something of a shock, that it was possible that King was already gone, that the weary, footsore remnants of the wild bunches up in Twin Buttes were already forming themselves back into bands without the presence of the big trumpeting stallion. He and Dixie might never see King again.

This worry kept returning to Ben more and more frequently, but he had promised himself that he would not go up to Twin Buttes, not any more until Tom Sample and his men had left. Whatever happened up there would have to happen without him, since he could not do anything about it anyway. His presence would only cause trouble.

A time came, however, when the hay was cut and in the windrows. There was nothing to do but wait for the sun to complete the process of curing so there would be no heating or molding in the stacks. "I guess I'll look up Tanger," Ben told his father at the breakfast table. "We'll be doing some riding pretty soon and I'll need him."

"A good idea," Vince said. "I haven't seen him since Dixie turned him out."

"I saw him a couple of times," Steve said. "He was up at the head of Fickle Creek with those two bay mares and their colts. I guess it was two or three weeks back. He'll probably be feeling pretty good, so watch out," he added with a grin.

"Don't worry," Ben said. "After Dixie rode him to school all winter, I guess I can stick on."

"Don't be too sure of that," Dixie said. "He's got plenty of life."

Ben saddled Inky at the barn and turned toward the creek, where the up-and-down canyon trail lay on the side opposite the fields. The gaucho was busy in the breaking pen and Ben, always interested in what the horse-trainer was doing, pulled up a minute to watch. The gaucho had a colt tied to the center snubbing post and was approaching him with the strangely padded sheepskin saddle which he had brought to the ranch and always rode. The colt rolled his eyes and flung his weight back against the rope. Gaucho's soft voice purred at the animal reassuringly and his movements were slow and unexciting. He stopped, eyed the colt a second, then said, "Hello, Ben. Is good morning, no?" When working with colts, Gaucho always had plenty of time.

"Yes," Ben said. "Say, isn't that the full brother to Pop's Buck horse?"

"Si."

Ben grinned and said, "He's liable to give you some trouble. It took Pop quite a while to get Buck under the saddle."

Gaucho grinned back. "He has—how you say it?—fire plenty, but he will no give trouble. First I make him tame, then I ride him."

"It's a good trick, if you can do it," Ben said.

"With him, I can do it," Gaucho replied. "Some horses, no. But with him, yes."

"Buck unloaded Pop twice," Ben said, warningly.

Gaucho's grin widened and he said, "El Señor Pop no make him tame first."

"No," Ben said, "I guess he didn't. Have you seen anything of Tanger lately?"

Gaucho thought, then said, "No. I no see Tanger since Dixie turn him out."

"I'm going to get him," Ben said. Then he had another thought. While they had been haying, Gaucho had done considerable riding. "Have you seen anything of any strange tracks up the canyon?"

"No." Gaucho shook his head.

"Well, I wish you'd watch out for some," Ben said. "Or, if you see anybody riding up that way, let me know."

Gaucho was silent a second, then said, "The black stallion, no? You are worry for him?"

"Well," Ben said. "I'd just kind of like to know what happens to him. You can understand that."

"Si," Gaucho said.

"I've got to be going now," Ben said and touched his heels to Inky's ribs. The gaucho knew of course how much it hurt him to lose King.

Ben kept Inky stepping steadily and turned into the mouth of Fickle Creek before the sun reached its mid-morning point. A mile or so up the canyon, where it widened into grassy meadows, he sighted some horses, the two bay mares and their colts that Steve had mentioned. Each of the mares had suckling colts and one yearling was still with them. Ben left the trail and rode over to them, expecting to find the chestnut Tanger nearby. But Tanger was nowhere to be seen, nor, when the mares and colts started to move away, did he come from the brush. Ben pulled up and waited, but Tanger did not appear. Presently Ben was forced to the conclusion that he was no longer with them. And that was unusual enough to make Ben worry. A horse could step in a badger hole and break his leg, or fall from a rock ledge. Or he might be tangled in the wire of that old fence someone had strung years ago across the head of the canyon. Something might have happened, and Tanger was much too good a horse to lose. Ben turned Inky up the canyon.

Although there were numerous horse tracks, most of them several weeks old or older, in the upper canyon, Ben found the half-buried strands of the old wire undisturbed. But still there was no sign of Tanger. Looking at the tracks, Ben recognized them as those of the mares and colts he had seen earlier. Then he saw another track that he knew as well as he knew the palm of his hand. Dixie had not expected Tanger to be loose so long, and she had not asked her father to pull off the chestnut's shoes, so the print of his round hoofs was made further evident by the iron shoes. Tanger had been here, just as Steve had said; but where was he now? The shod tracks were weeks old.

Ben had long known the importance of ground sign as a source of information for riders. He had made a study of tracks and trails, including those of the wild animals, such as badgers, coyotes and antelope, as well as those of horses and cows. Now he began to cast about in the floor of the upper canyon, watching for sign. The tracks were all hopelessly mingled in the meadow area and Ben made his circle still wider. Presently he came to a section where the shod prints were more numerous and he held to this, working his way carefully. Tanger had obviously fed above the other horses a few days. Ben kept working the sign and after a time he found himself in the head of the canyon, where the ground sloped up steeply toward the Fickle Flats country. Tack stock seldom ranged up there, for the feed was sparse at the western edge of the Flats, but Ben knew that he could do nothing less than follow Tanger's trail. Even though it was days old, Tanger was somewhere at the end of it.

He put Inky to the climb. It was steep here and the footing was made difficult by the rocks and boulders. Ben let Inky take his time and halted him at regular intervals for wind. Tanger's tracks showed that he too had made the climb in leisurely fashion, pausing frequently to crop down bunches of grass.

It was after the noon hour when Ben topped out on Fickle Flats. A careful survey from his stirrups failed to reveal any horse or horses, so Ben turned his attention back to Tanger's tracks. The trail meandered here and there for a while then, to Ben's surprise, turned in a straight line into the Fickle country. It was strange that Tanger would leave his accustomed range. Ben searched for other tracks, to determine whether the horse had been led or driven, but could find none. Yet Tanger went so straight that Ben almost suspected that he was being ridden. The horse was gentle, and a man on foot could have caught him. But Ben did not remember seeing any man tracks.

He rode on into the brush and had gone less than half a mile when the mystery was solved. The shod prints joined those of a number of other horses, all unshod, and the whole mass moved slowly across the country, grazing on the scattered grass. "Well!" Ben said to himself. "What do you know about that?" Tanger, his old gentle Tanger horse, ranch raised and broken by the gaucho, had joined a wild bunch. After feeding up as far as Fickle Flats, Tanger had seen a herd of wild horses in the brush and, ready then for the company of his own kind, had decided to go to them instead of returning to the Tack mares in the canyon. Ben knew that this happened once in a while when ranch horses strayed, as Tanger had done, beyond their customary range. More than once he had seen branded horses running in the wild bunches, usually mares which the stallion welcomed and sometimes even went out of his way to acquire. That was another score which the stockmen had against the wild stallions. Some stallions would not permit geldings in their bands, but others tolerated them, and Ben could find no evidence that the leader of this particular herd had made any protest at Tanger's arrival. Probably the band had been feeding its way up from the river breaks and the stallion had not been at the height of his belligerency. Whatever had happened, it was clear to Ben now that Tanger had joined a wild bunch.

Ben became immediately concerned. Tanger was his own horse, picked with his father's permission from Tack's crop of three-year-old colts two years before, and he had a strong affection for the animal. But for the past year he had done most of his riding on Inky, whom he had broken and trained himself and who was a year younger than Tanger. A ranch rider needs a string of several good horses, and Ben had no intention of losing Tanger, but he knew that a horse, even one as gentle and well-trained as the chestnut, often became almost impossible to catch after he had run for a time with the spooky wild ones. He debated whether to go back and tell his father what had happened or to continue on Tanger's trail himself, and presently decided upon the latter course, for the time being. He still had a good part of the afternoon left and his father, busy and set against wild horses anyway, would be displeased.

Ben knew that to follow the old winding trail would take too much time, so he laid a course direct across Fickle Flats to Juniper Springs. Juniper Springs was a regular watering place for the wild bunches and Ben thought that if he had a little luck, he might find Tanger in that vicinity. With a little more luck, he might even catch him.

It was a two-hour ride to Juniper and when Ben arrived he found the water hole deserted. He rode in to it anyway, knowing that Inky would appreciate a drink. Tracks were thick in the damp earth at the edge of the water and he saw a number that had been made by shod horses. He dismounted to examine one of these closely and found that it was not Tanger's. Ben straightened with a frown on his face. Either other shod horses were running with the wild bands or some rider had been there. Ben remembered then that he was in the area where Tom Sample was running the wild horses, or at least had been. That track was probably left by Tom himself or one of his riders.

Ben looked around, feeling slightly guilty. He had not intended to come here while Tom was after King, knowing well enough that Tom would resent his presence. Still, he felt that he had good reason to come; he had a horse up there and a man certainly had the right to catch his own horse. He was glad however, as he mounted Inky, that there was no one around to see him. Of course, they might see Inky's tracks and conclude that a strange rider had been there, but he did not think it likely. A man riding in the dust of a wild bunch does not pay much attention to ground sign.

Leaving Juniper, Ben headed directly west, intending to intersect the Three Deck trail and follow it as the nearest way to the ranch. It was too late now to search any farther for Tanger. By the time he reached Tack it would be nearing sundown and having missed the noon meal, he fully intended to be there for supper. Tanger would have to wait till another day.

Ben had proceeded about three miles when he noticed a rise of dust in front of him and to the right. He studied it as he rode and came to the conclusion that it was made by horses, a number of them, and moving at a good pace. Tom Sample and his runners were still in Twin Buttes, still after the wild horses. Ben felt a small thrill of pleasure. Tom had not caught them yet. King was still running the high country, still in control of his band.

"Good old King," Ben said to himself, then went on to his horse, "that old pop of yours is just a lot of horse, Inky. He's giving Tom Sample plenty of trouble."

A small hope even flickered in Ben; Tom might not catch the stallion. But he knew his hope was futile. With Tom's grain-fed horses and plenty of riders, it was merely a matter of time.

Ben continued to watch the dust. It did not seem to move but increased in size, and Ben realized that the wild horses were headed almost straight in his direction, probably to go into Juniper Springs for water. They would get little water, Ben knew, for the rider behind would whip up his mount and drive them on before they had time to drink. However, if they held their present direction, they would pass quite close to him, on the right. When they saw him they would spook away to the east, and the runner following them would know they had sighted something unusual. If he paused to investigate . . . Ben decided that the best thing he could do was to get under cover, out of sight. Tom Sample would insist that he had spooked the horses on purpose, to make them more difficult to catch.

There were three things Ben considered doing: He could turn directly west and urge Inky to a gallop and thus be out of sight by the time the wild horses arrived; or he could get into the old dry arroyo to his left and dismount; or he could hide, horse and all, in the clump of stunted juniper on the little rise that he had just passed. After a few seconds of thought, Ben turned back to the junipers. To ride west would cause him to go several miles out of his way, and he dismissed the arroyo because he wanted to be where he could see.

Ben dismounted in the junipers and glanced around. This would serve his purpose. Inky's dark body would not be noticeable and Ben could watch the progress of the chase through the twisted branches. He found himself somewhat excited by the thought that he might see King again.

The streamer of dust now stood high above the brush and after a few minutes Ben saw a dark spot at the base of it, and another and another. They were horses. More horses appeared and they came on toward Ben. He rose and put his hand on Inky's nose, to keep the horse from whinnying. Inky had run with the wild bunch and the sight of these horses might excite him.

After a time the animal in the lead was close enough for Ben to identify, and then he knew without question that it was King's band. This old bay mare, with a ragged white spot in her forehead, almost always ran at the head of King's band. And there was another one Ben recognized, the paint mare with the broad band of white across her shoulders. She had appeared in King's bunch three years before and had been with him ever since. Undersized but smart and tough, she had, Ben suspected, escaped from the Indian reservation which lay to the southeast.

Inky threw his short black ears forward and Ben tightened his grip on the horse's nostrils. A neigh would be certain to draw the wild horses' attention, and possibly that of the rider behind them.

[98]

Holding a straight course to Juniper Springs, the lead mare passed Ben's hiding place at a distance of not more than two hundred yards and somewhat below him. Even without his glasses, he could see her clearly. She, like those behind her, was moving at a gallop, but it was a slow and weary gait and occasionally she dropped to a trot. Ben had no way of telling how long the runners had been after them, but obviously it was days. Already the suckling colts had dropped out and were scattered across the desert. After a couple of days of hard running, the colts began to drop out and usually their mothers, defying the stallion's efforts to drive them on, would stop with them. But these were not the horses the runners wanted, so they paid no attention to them. Sometimes, when the herd came around again, the colts and mares would rejoin it and run again until their sore feet and weary legs would no longer carry them.

But what was that? Ben suddenly leaned forward, his eyes on a running form down in the dust—a trim chestnut. Tanger? It was Tanger. Ben knew he could not be mistaken. He had an impulse to open his mouth and yell the horse's name, forgetting that at that distance and in the rumble of hoofs Tanger could not possibly hear him. The wild excitement of the run was in Tanger now, and as long as this anxiety and fright lasted he would remain, for comfort and a sense of security, with the other horses.

Ben was shocked by his discovery. Tanger was in a wild bunch, being run like any other wild horse. Of course, when Tom Sample and his men found the Tack brand on him they would release him. They would not dare do otherwise. But Ben was worried. Tom had no right to be running his horse. On the other hand, Tom would maintain that Tanger had no right to be with a wild bunch.

Ben's mind was so busy with his problem that he was not prepared for the flurry of hoofs and the emergence out of the dust below of a big black stallion. A single glance however told him that it was King—King, bringing up the rear where the danger was and moving with a strong stride. But Ben could tell that the big horse was tired. He went on, following the others, with an occasional toss of his head to look behind. Ben knew from his own experience that King still had a lot of run left in him, could still, if the occasion demanded, put on a burst of speed that would tax most of Tom Sample's saddle horses. But in the end all this splendid endurance would be a dismal waste.

Ben stayed in his position until the rider passed. It was Pearly Maunderland, riding a big sorrel horse that obviously had entered the chase only a short time back. Pearly made no effort to draw up to the wild horses; his job was merely to keep them moving, wear down their strength and make them sore footed. The big push, the climax of the run, would come later.

After Maunderland had passed, Ben mounted Inky and turned him in the direction of the Three Deck trail. And as Ben rode, there was an unhappy frown on his face.

CHAPTER NINE

"Did you find Tanger?" Steve asked casually at the supper table.

"Yes, I found him," Ben said. He was trying to make up for the meal he had missed.

"Did you bring him in?" Dixie wanted to know.

"No."

"Why not?"

"Couldn't catch him. He was running with some other horses and they were spooky."

"Why didn't you run the whole bunch in?" his father asked.

"Oh, I didn't think it was worth it," Ben said. "I can go back and get him later."

Ben had decided that he would not tell his father that Tanger was with the wild bunch, being run by Tom Sample and his men. He would not tell him yet, anyway. He did not know just what his father's reaction might be. As a rule, horse-runners who caught a branded horse either turned it back to the range or, if it was convenient, took it to the ranch that owned it. Sometimes they took it to the nearest ranch and informed the owner that it was there, so he could come after it. But Ben had no confidence in Tom Sample and his men. He was certain they would not take Tanger back to town; they had too much respect for the law and his father's strong temper to do that. But they might mistreat and abuse the horse, taking the opportunity to vent their spite against Ben; they might release him on a distant part of the range where months would go by before Ben could find him; or they might, if by chance they could catch Tanger, use him to run the wild horses. Tanger, in Ben's opinion, was a better horse than any they had in their saddle strings, and he believed that Tom or Pearly, if they thought they would not be detected, would not hesitate to run his legs off. Ben knew well enough that a good horse could be ruined by an inconsiderate rider who was after a wild bunch. But the thought that his own horse might be used to catch King irritated Ben most of all.

But Ben's answers at the table were too casual to suit Dixie. After supper, when they had gathered in the living room, she caught Ben's eye, jerked her head and went through the kitchen and out the back door. Ben knew that he had best humor her, so he followed a few minutes later. She was at the main corral, leaning on the fence.

"What do you want?" Ben said gruffly, to let her know he was not particularly pleased at being called out of the house.

"What happened?" she said. "Why didn't you bring Tanger in?"

"Couldn't catch him?" Ben said.

"Why?" she insisted. "He's easy to catch. All you have to do is walk right up to him. I can catch him anywhere."

"He was running with some other horses and they spooked," Ben said.

"Those bay mares? Don't tell me that."

"Gee whiz, Dix. I tell you they were running. I didn't get close to them. You know how horses are when they get started running, even gentle ones."

It was not too dark for her to see his face and she looked at him keenly for several seconds, then said, "You were up in Twin Buttes?"

"I was just looking for Tanger," Ben said. "All I did was follow him."

"You were up there?"

"Could I help it if Tanger took a notion to go up in Fickle Flats?"

"It was wild horses that he was running with," she said. "That's the reason you couldn't catch him?"

"Yes," Ben admitted angrily.

"King's bunch?"

"Yes."

"And Tom Sample was after them?"

"Pearly Maunderland was."

"Relaying them?"

"Yes."

"How'd they look?"

"Tired. The suckling colts had all dropped out."

She was silent a second, then said, "Did you see King?"

"Yes. He's still strong."

"I hope they don't get him," she said. "I hope he gets away."

"They will," Ben said. "They'll keep on till they do."

"Darn it! I wish something would happen."

"What can?"

Dixie had no answer for that, and presently she said, "What about Tanger? What are you going to do about him?"

"I don't know," he admitted.

"You can't catch him," she said, "not as long as he's running with the band and Tom keeps them spooked."

Ben knew she was right.

"If there were just some way to cut him out, to get him away from the others!" she said.

"How?" he asked.

She shrugged, having no answer.

"If they can catch him," Ben said presently, "they'll use him. I don't like that. I don't want Tom Sample or Pearly Maunderland riding one of my horses."

"No," she agreed with an emphatic nod of her head. Then she added, "I think you should tell Pop."

Ben considered that a long time, but finally shook his head. "No, he wouldn't do anything. You know how he is. And he wouldn't let me do anything."

She said, "What're you going to do? What can you do?"

"I don't know," he said. "I'm trying to think of something. I'm not going to have Tom Sample using Tanger, not if I can keep him from it."

"I'll help you," she said.

"How can you help me?"

"I don't know, but I will."

"Don't you do anything without telling me," Ben warned seriously.

"I helped you catch King the other time," she said.

"Yes, but this is different. We've got to watch out for Tom Sample and Pearly Maunderland."

"Pooh on them," she said. "I'm not afraid of them."

"I'm not either," he said, "but Pop won't let us interfere with their rights. You know that."

"They've got no right to Tanger, not even to run him," she replied. "He's a branded horse."

"Yes, but he's got no right to be in the wild band," Ben said.

"Yes, but how does he know that? He doesn't know he hasn't got any business up there. It's up to us to look out for him."

"Yes," Ben agreed, strengthened by her argument. "We've got to do something, Dix. I'll think of something."

Ben went to bed that night still trying to think of something, something they could do to save Tanger from a lot of useless running and from possibly being ridden by Tom Sample or his men. He got up the next morning still trying to think, and realized that he had not got very far.

"Are you going back after Tanger today, Ben?" his father asked at the breakfast table.

"No," Ben said. Tanger was a good day's ride from Tack. "I'll get back to him in a day or two," Ben added.

"Then maybe you'd better take the wagon and go up and get a load of wood," Vince said. "We can start laying up some for winter."

"All right," Ben said. That was not what he had had in mind, but it would do. He could think as well while gathering wood as doing anything else, and it would not hurt Inky to have a day's rest.

Ben worked hard and brought two loads of mountain mahogany down from a flank of Crystal Mountain. The mahogany was brittle and hard to cut but his mother liked it even better than coal for the kitchen stove.

As he came down the slope with his load of crooked limbs, Ben could look up and see Three Deck trail almost all the way to the top. He had plenty of time to think, but the thinking seemed to get him nowhere. He always came back to the same place, to the knowledge that it was not Tom Sample's fault that Tanger was up in Twin Buttes. So what could he, Ben, do about it? But from Dixie, the night before, had come the germ of an idea. And during the day, since he could think of nothing else, Ben turned the thought over and over in his mind. If, as Dixie had pointed out, they could just get Tanger separated from the bunch, then they could catch him. Once he realized who they were, Tanger would let either one of them, or almost anyone else, walk up to him, especially if they, as Pop put it, "made a noise like a pan of oats."

To cut a single horse out of a wild band was a difficult task; the horse, having a natural sense of security in numbers, frequently became panic stricken and would try its best to get back. But it could be done. Ben and Dixie and the gaucho had cut King out of his band, and a stallion is the hardest of all to separate. That was what they would have to do with Tanger. But Tom Sample complicated the matter.

Ben thought about telling the gaucho and getting him to help, then decided against it. The gaucho had thrown a knife at Pearly Maunderland once before, when Pearly was in the act of pulling a gun, and if they happened to meet again in Twin Buttes, trouble was certain. Ben knew however that he would need help, and that night at the supper table, when Dixie was listening, he said, "I think I'll go after Tanger in the morning, Pop."

"I'll go with you," Dixie said quickly. "I can help you catch him if he gives you any trouble."

"I'll start early and I'll likely be gone all day," Ben said.

"I'll fix us a lunch," Dixie said. "May I ride Listo, Gaucho?"

"Si, for ciertamenta," the gaucho answered, with a pleased smile. "Listo, she need it."

"Bring in my Sauce horse, if you see him," Steve said. "I'm going to turn old Pickett out for a while."

Shadows still lay in Crystal Creek Canyon when Ben and Dixie forded the creek and turned their horses up Three Deck trail. The air was cool and clean, and the black gelding and the sand-colored mare stepped out briskly. Ben had his binoculars tied to the fork of his saddle, opposite his rope. The flat canteen, its fabric cover wet and dripping, hung on the left side also. Their lunch was tied behind the cantle of Dixie's saddle. Dixie's light saddle had been made especially for her, and she rode with an unconscious ease and assurance, neither needing nor expecting any unusual consideration because she was a girl.

Ben turned in his saddle and frowned. "I wish you hadn't brought that mare," he said.

"Why?"

"Pearly Maunderland claimed she was his once. Remember? That was the reason he tried to pull a gun on the gaucho."

"Yes, but Gaucho proved she wasn't."

"He did as far as we're concerned," Ben said. "But Pearly hasn't forgotten it. He'd still like to have her, and he'd like to get even with Gaucho."

"He won't get her," Dixie said emphatically.

"No, but he'd like to. I wish you hadn't brought her."

A hundred yards farther on, Dixie said, "Are we going to see Pearly?"

"No, but we might run into him or some of Tom's men. I don't intend to, but you never can tell."

"What're we going to do? How're we going to work it?"

"It all depends," Ben said. "We'll see how we find them; maybe we'll have some luck."

"What kind of luck?" she said.

"Well," Ben said, "I'm figuring on cutting Tanger out of the wild bunch. Once we get him off by himself, we can catch him. I brought along some oats."

"So that's what's in that sack? How're you going to do it without being seen? That's what I want to know."

"I don't know," Ben said. "That's where the luck will come in."

When they reached the high country, Ben turned Inky's nose directly toward the ridge he had calculated would be passed by King and his band sometime during the afternoon.

On the ridge, Ben found a clump of juniper that offered some shade and dismounted. He took out his binoculars and sat down on a convenient rock. First he studied the country to the north and east.

"What's that over there?" Dixie said. "Looks like dust."

"It is," Ben said. He focused the glasses on it and after several seconds said, "It's probably them. It's too far away to tell for sure."

"What else would be raising a dust like that?"

Ben shook his head. "Loosen the cinches. We'll wait here."

An hour later the dust was approaching Basin Lake. Ben watched it carefully. "They're not going in," he said presently.

"Tom's got his camp there," Dixie said.

"Yes."

At that distance, the dust cloud moved slowly, rising from a point. The light wind came from the west and the dust drifted slowly eastward.

Shortly after the dust had passed Basin Lake, there was

a fresh thickening of it and Ben said, "A new rider is taking over."

"Can you see him? Let me see," Dixie said, taking the glasses.

"He's back in the dust," Ben said. "You can't see him."

"I can see the horses," Dixie said. "Get our lunch and bring the water. We might as well eat while we've got time."

The dust cloud grew in size and after a time they could see the lead horses without the assistance of the glasses. Ben got to his feet and said, "Come on. Let's get ready." He tightened the saddle cinches, mounted, and rode south down the slope. Where the ground flattened, he turned west and headed for the jumble of big broken boulders at the point of the ridge. He rode in among these, halted, and looked at Dixie. "You ready?" he said.

She nodded, excitement bright in her eyes.

"All right," Ben said. "They'll pass pretty close. Tanger will likely be running about the center, a little to one side or the other. We'll go in and find him. They'll break and scatter when we first hit them and maybe we can turn Tanger east. If we do, keep him moving. Don't let him turn back and don't stop for anything. Do you understand?"

"You bet," she said.

The dust cloud was close now and Dixie said, "There's King's old lead mare out in front. She's smart. Tom Sample won't get them in a trap, not with her leading."

"Let her get past," Ben said. "We want to hit them just about the middle."

The horses were closing up, coming at a good trot. In addition to the bay mare with the white splash in her face they could see a number of other horses, running either to her left or right. Sensing that something was about to happen, Inky and Listo began to fidget and push at the reins for slack. The bay mare went past, and the dark forms of the other horses trotted after her in the dust.

"There's Tanger," Dixie said in a low voice. "I see him."

"Let's go," Ben said, loosening his reins.

Inky left the rocks at a fast gallop. Ben headed him into the dust ahead of the chestnut. Ben jerked his rope loose; there might be a chance for a throw. The horses in the dust broke the steady rhythm of their stride and for an instant were confused. Then, as Ben had foreseen, they wheeled east and ran with all the speed still remaining in their tired bodies.

Ben was in the dust. Off to the right he could hear Dixie's high-pitched, "Yyeeeeeoooo!" He swerved more to the left, hoping they could get Tanger between them. Inky was running now, neck stretched and hoofs pounding the ground. Half a dozen horses were running through the brush ahead of Ben, Tanger among them. Recovering from their first fright, they began to circle south, hoping to get back to the band. Behind them the other wild horses, bewildered and half blinded by the dust, were running in a dozen different directions. Ben let Inky stretch, and the horses in front, seeing that he would head them, suddenly halted, then wheeled and rushed back into the swirling dust behind them. Ben brought Inky around and raced back, seeking to hold the little bunch clear, but the dust was like a curtain through which the dark forms of horses plunged and galloped on all sides. Ben lost sight of Tanger and could not find him again.

Dixie appeared out of the haze. "Where's Tanger?" Ben shouted at her.

"This way," she answered and was gone, shaking her reins in Listo's ears.

Ben rode after her. A wild horse thundered at his side for a few seconds before discovering him and shying away. Ben couldn't find Tanger and he couldn't find Dixie. By the sound of the hoofs he knew that most of the wild bunch had filtered past him. He knew too that Tanger had escaped, so he rode out of the dust and halted Inky. A big black form pounded up, saw Ben and shied around him with an angry snort. King! Ben could hardly keep from clapping his heels to Inky's flanks. His rope was ready and he could catch King; he was somehow certain of it. A quick dash— But what good would it do? He would have a rope full of trouble and Tom Sample would take the stallion.

"Whoa, Ink," Ben said.

King went on, galloping with lengthened stride. He shied again and Ben knew the stallion had become aware of Dixie, somewhere in the dust. Ben waited, watched, and soon saw Dixie.

There was a beat of hoofs in the other direction and Ben turned to see a rider coming. It was Tom Sample's man, of course. Ben wished suddenly that they were out of there, but it was too late then.

"What do you think you're doing?" the man cried angrily, bringing his horse to a halt. It was Pearly Maunderland.

"I'm waiting for my sister," Ben said.

"What do you mean, bustin' into that bunch?" Maunderland said. "I'm runnin' them."

The man's belligerent manner angered Ben and he said, "You're running one of mine, and I don't like it."

Maunderland's little eyes narrowed and he said, "That stud's not yours, and he never has been. You know that."

"I'm not talking about him."

"Then, what are you talkin' about?"

"There's a chestnut gelding in there with a Tack brand. If you'd ever been close to them you'd have seen it."

"I don't believe it," Maunderland said.

By now Dixie had ridden up. "That doesn't matter," she said. "He's there."

She made little attempt to hide her likes and dislikes, and she never had liked Pearly Maunderland.

Pearly thought a minute, then said, "Is he that colt you rode up here before?"

"Yes," Ben said. He had been riding Tanger that summer two years ago.

"Well, what's he doing in a wild bunch?"

"He strayed."

"Then I guess that's just his hard luck," Pearly said. "We won't stop running wild horses just because there's a stray in the bunch. You're crazy."

"I'm not asking you to," Ben said. "All I want you to do is give me a chance to catch him, to get him out."

"I should say not. Look what you've done now; they're scattered all over the country."

"They'll get back together, and you know it," Dixie said.

"But we'll have to wait," Maunderland said. "That'll give them time to rest."

"I wish they had sense enough to stay scattered," Dixie said. "Then you'd never get them."

"You'd like that, wouldn't you?" the man said, tauntingly.

"They're not scattered much," Ben said. "We just tried to cut Tanger out."

"But you couldn't do it?"

"No, the dust was too thick."

"If you'd let them stop a while—" Dixie said hopefully.

"Just when we've about got them run down?" Maunderland said. "Not much. Where'd you get that mare? She looks like one that was stole from me."

"You know where I got her," Dixie said. "And you know who owns her. The only time she was ever stolen was from him."

"That little spic!" Maunderland said. "Keep him away from me. Tell him I said he had better not come up here."

"Come on, Dix, let's go," Ben said.

"And you keep away from this wild bunch while we're running them," the man went on angrily. "Stay plumb away from them. If you bust into them again, there's going to be trouble. Hear me?"

"If you hurt my horse, there's going to be trouble. too." Ben said earnestly. "Don't even put a rope on him."

"Then keep him out of the way," the man said.

Ben turned his horse and rode off, headed in the direction of Three Deck. He heard Dixie coming behind him and presently she was up beside him. She turned her head and looked back, but Ben kept looking straight ahead.

"Well," Dixie said, after a time, "that didn't turn out so good."

"No," Ben admitted dismally.

CHAPTER TEN

"GET YOUR horse, Ben?"

They were sitting around the supper table and the room was full of the smells of good food and kitchen warmth. A gasoline lamp hanging from the ceiling threw its white light against the yellow-tinted walls and down on the dishes and glasses and knives and forks and the checkered tablecloth. Vince Darby sat at the head of the table, Steve and the gaucho were along one side; Mom was at the other end, and around the corner from her was Dixie's place. Ben sat on that side too, directly across from Steve. Riding and work in the open created strong appetites, and meals at Tack were important affairs, with the chief attention on the food. The conversation was usually light and casual, and that was the manner in which Ben tried to pass off his father's question.

"No sir," Ben said, grinning with what he hoped was the proper degree of feigned embarrassment. "We jumped him, but he cleaned us."

"Got away from you, eh?" Vince said.

"Mean to say the both of you couldn't head him?" Steve said.

"Oh, I guess we could have, if we had stayed after him long enough," Ben said. "I'm in no hurry for him anyway, and he got out in front of us."

"He can run," Dixie said.

"Yes," Steve said, "but usually he tries to find out what you've got in your pockets first. You must have been pretty dumb."

"We'll get him," Ben said cheerfully.

"Where'd you find him?" Vince said.

"Up Fickle—way up," Ben said, telling himself that it was way up. "We didn't see anything of Sauce, Steve."

"I think he's on the west slope," Steve said. "I'll ride down that way tomorrow and have a look. If I see Tanger, I'll bring him in."

"Okay," Ben said.

"What're you going to do tomorrow, Ben?" Dixie asked.

"Ben can help me," his father said. "You can, too. Cattle is getting too thick in Wolf Creek. We'll move most of the steers out. I want to save that feed for fall."

Starting high in the Wolf Creek breaks the next morning, Ben and his father and Dixie made their drag down the creek, Ben riding the south slopes and Vince the north, with Dixie in the center. They went into the gulches and ravines and started the fat white-faced cows and kept them moving. Working naturally down the slopes, the animals gathered before Dixie, who made sure that none got behind her. At the mouth of the creek they had a sizable herd.

Dixie held them while Vince and Ben cut out a few cows which, because they had young calves, were to be left. They took the rest across Crystal Canyon and pushed them up the brushy slope of the mountain. The grass up here was not so good as in the creek bottoms and now, during the summer, was the time to harvest it.

But as Ben rode, his mind was not on the cows. It was back up in Twin Buttes, where a band of footsore, weary horses was raising a banner of dust before relentless riders. A few days of running, without time to graze and only hurried sups of water, would be all that was needed. Tom Sample and his riders could turn them into a trap or take them with ropes. Of course, Tom had to have King, and he would be the hardest one to get. He would go as long as his legs would carry him, and after that he would fight the ropes until they choked him down. There would not be many of the horses left running when Tom finally caught King, not unless Tom managed to get them into a trap. But Ben was certain Tanger would be there. With shoes to protect his feet and having been grain fed all winter, Tanger would stand the ordeal better than the wild horses. Ben was glad of that. Tanger would come through all right, if . . . if Tom Sample and Pearly Maunderland did not do something to him. Ben could not help worrying.

Steve was at the big corral when Ben and Vince and Dixie arrived back at the ranch in the late afternoon. Sauce and a couple of colts were in the corral and Steve was there with his rope. The big sorrel was full of snort and tricks after having run loose so long, and Vince and Dixie and Ben pulled up at the fence to watch.

"You're liable to have your hands full, Steve," Dixie called, happily anticipating the excitement.

Steve did not reply, and his throw, when he made it, was quick and sure. He dug his heels into the beaten earth and brought Sauce around at the end of the rope. Sauce snorted and reared. Steve advanced toward him, moving slowly, hand over hand, along the rope. "Whoa, boy. Easy, boy," Steve said, his voice low and calm. The horse stood and presently Steve was rubbing his nose. A few seconds of that, and Steve made a loop around the horse's jaws with the rope, then turned to the fence where his saddle and bridle were on the top rail. Sauce followed.

"Want me to help you saddle him?" Ben asked.

"No," Steve said.

Sauce protested briefly against the hackamore and shivered when Steve put up the blanket and then the saddle. He shied away when Steve reached under for the cinch, but Steve had it and ran the latigo through the ring. A noticeable hump came in Sauce's back as Steve pulled the cinch tight and made the tie.

"He hasn't been ridden much," Vince said, a quiet warning in his voice.

"That knot in his back is liable to unravel," Dixie chirped.

Steve looked up at them and grinned. "He's not half as bad as he thinks he is," he said, and with the flat of his hand he hit Sauce a strong blow on the ribs to make the horse release the wind he was holding in his lungs against the cinch pressure. Sauce snorted and swung around. "There, that's better," Steve told him and retightened the cinch.

"Climb on," Dixie urged.

Steve made a face at her. He turned and led Sauce by the hackamore reins, led him around the big corral twice, letting him get used to the feel of the saddle. Then back in front of them he stopped, slapped the horse easily on the shoulder, and put the reins over his head. Catching the reins up tight, and taking a handful of mane as a precaution, Steve turned the stirrup to receive his foot, said, "Whoa, Sauce," and slowly lifted himself into the saddle. His foot found the right stirrup and he was ready. The horse's body sunk into a crouch, hair-triggered on the muscles of his powerful hind quarters. That was the critical instant. "Easy, boy. Easy," Steve said. He waited a few seconds, then eased the rein tension. Sauce's lungs had been charged for action, but now the breath came out through his nostrils with a sound loud enough for Dixie and Ben and their father to hear. He took a step forward.

"Shucks," Dixie said.

Steve looked over at them and said, "Want me to give him his head?"

"No," Vince said. "There's no use in letting him buck." Vince turned to the barn to unsaddle.

Steve rode around the corral and, as he came back, said, "I didn't see anything of Tanger, Ben. Looks as if he's left Fickle Creek."

The next day was an uneasy one for Ben. The following morning, as soon as he had finished his breakfast, he went back upstairs and got his binoculars and hid them in the front of his shirt. He had just finished saddling Inky in the runway behind the stalls when Dixie came in, carrying her bridle and saddle. She did not speak to him, but went into Listo's stall.

"Where're you going?" Ben said, not pleased.

"Riding," she said.

"Where to?"

"Up in Twin Buttes."

"Twin Buttes? Who said you could go up there?"

"No one. Who said you could?"

"I didn't say I was going up there."

"Oh, yeah?" she said. "What have you got inside your shirt?"

Color mounted in Ben's face. "That doesn't mean I'm going to Twin Buttes," he said. "I could be going anywhere."

She backed the mare out of the stall and said, "Let's get started. Pop'll be coming pretty soon and he might ask questions."

Ben knew it was useless to argue any longer. He mounted Inky and led the way out the back door of the runway. They paused at the creek to let the horses drink, then turned downstream to the intersection with Three Deck trail.

High on the ridge, Dixie said, "What have you got in mind, Ben? What are you going to do?"

Ben shook his head. "Nothing. I just want to see . . . I want to make certain Tanger's all right."

"Are you going to try to cut him out of the bunch again?"

"No. If we do that, Tom Sample will go down to see Pop. You know what that'll mean. Pop will stop us from coming up here."

"You're just going to let them keep running your horse?" she said, disapprovingly.

"I can't do anything else. But he'll be all right; he has shoes on—at least, he did have—and he's in good shape. Running won't be as tough on him as on the others."

"It'll be tough, if Pearly Maunderland can make it tough," she said.

"Yes," Ben said. "I guess Tom and Pearly wouldn't mind seeing something happen to him, because he's my horse. That's the reason I decided to come up today. If I can find out when they figure to start catching, I'll be there. I'll be there to get Tanger, whether Tom likes it or not."

"How're you going to find out?"

"I don't know—yet. By watching, maybe. Maybe I can tell just about how much longer the wild horses will run. Tanger'll quit when they do. He'll be easy to catch then."

"What if they trap them?"

"I'll find it," Ben said. "I'll find the trap."

Dixie was thoughtful, then said, "It wouldn't do any good to ask Tom. He wouldn't tell us what he's got in mind."

"No," Ben agreed. "We'll have to find out for ourselves. And I'm going to, if I have to come back up here every day. I want to be there to get Tanger."

"Me, too," she said.

"Oh, there's no use of your coming," he said.

"That's what you think," she said.

Reaching the top of Three Deck, Ben headed as usual for Gailey Ridge, where he could make a survey of the surrounding country. It did not take them long to find the dust, but it was not where Ben had expected it to be. It was way out in Standing Rock Basin.

Ben frowned and said, "Something's happened."

"What?" Dixie said.

"I don't know, but something. They should be up close to Little Butte by now."

"Maybe something happened to the rider?" Dixie said hopefully. "Maybe his horse fell with him, stepped in a hole or something?"

Ben shook his head. "They're too smart for that. But something has happened. I wish I knew what it was."

Dixie took the glasses and put them on the distant dust cloud. Presently she said, "It's too far to see anything."

"They're still running them," Ben said, "or they wouldn't be raising that dust."

"Well," said Dixie, disappointed, "they won't be back around here until late tomorrow. We won't get to see them."

Ben took the glasses and turned them to the long stretch

of rolling country which lay to the north of Gailey. After a time he nodded his head and said, "I see him."

"See who?"

"The rider. He's headed for Little Butte. He'll pick them up there and bring them on around."

"Where? Let me see." Dixie took the glasses, looked for several seconds, then said, "I can't tell who he is."

"He's one of Tom's riders. You can bet on that." Ben took the glasses and turned them back on the dust cloud. Presently he lowered them and offered them to Dixie.

Dixie shook her head, knowing it was useless. "I wish you'd brought some lunch," she said.

"Why didn't you?" Ben said. "You're the one who's always hungry."

"You always eat the most," she said. "We might as well head back. We won't see anything today."

But Ben was still perplexed. "I sure wish I knew what happened."

"We could ride to Basin Lake," Dixie said. "Maybe Tom would tell us."

"No," Ben said. "They won't tell us anything."

"Well, there's no use in just sitting here," Dixie said.

Ben did not reply. He dug his heel into the ground for several minutes, then got up and turned to the horses. He mounted and turned down the south slope of the ridge.

"Where're you going?" Dixie wanted to know as she followed him.

"Standing Rock. There's something over there I want to have a look at."

"What?"

"A sink."

"Which one?"

"The one where Tom trapped King's band before."

"What do you want to look at it for?" Dixie said. "There're no horses in it. We know where they are."

"I just want to see it," Ben said.

They approached the little canyon from the west side. A hundred yards from the edge, Ben dismounted, handed his reins to Dixie, and told her to wait while he went forward on foot. He approached the rim cautiously, looked down and then straightened up. Dixie rode forward and said, "I told you there wouldn't be any horses here."

"There might have been," Ben said. "They've fixed the fence."

The lower fence, the one King had broken through before, stretched across the canyon below them and fresh new juniper poles showed where it had been repaired.

"They raised it at the big rock," Ben said. "They know how King got out before."

"They're going to try to get him in here again?" Dixie asked.

"Maybe," Ben said, still frowning. "Maybe they've already tried."

"What makes you think so?"

"Something happened," Ben said. He was still scanning the fence and the bottom area between the steep rock walls.

"Well, they didn't get them," Dixie said.

"No," Ben said. "Something happened."

Dixie kept silent, and after a few minutes Ben turned and mounted his horse. He started north, along the rim of the canyon.

"We might as well swing by Juniper Springs and water our horses," Dixie said.

Ben held to his direction. "I want to have a look up here," he said.

They came to the place where the upper fence had been. It had been taken down and the poles were piled neatly against the far wall. Ben nodded and said, "They sure planned to get them in here. It wouldn't take long to get that fence up again."

"But they won't be back around here before tomorrow night," Dixie said impatiently.

Ben rode on along the rim, past the place where it disappeared into the ground, and on into the brush. He kept watching the ground and after a time he halted at a jumble of fresh sign.

"Something happened here," he said to Dixie.

She said, "I don't see anything but a lot of horse tracks."

"They jumped them here," Ben said. "They jumped them here yesterday afternoon and tried to turn them into the trap."

"But they wouldn't go," Dixie said, pleased.

"No," Ben said. "And they got some rest. The runners let up on them a while so they would get back together. That's what happened, Dix."

"I'm glad they got away," she said.

"I am, too," Ben said. "I guess that'll show Tom he's dealing with some pretty smart horses. But," he went on gloomily, "he's still after them. He'll get them."

Dixie had been looking about and now she said, "What's that—over there?"

"Where?"

She pointed at a dark object in the brush.

Ben took out his glasses and put them up to his eyes. "It's a horse," he said.

"Lying down?" she said.

"Yes, I guess so." Ben lifted his reins and headed toward the animal. "It's probably too sore footed to stand," he said.

Dixie rode with him, and soon they could see that it was a bay horse, lying on its side. "It looks as if it's dead," Dixie said presently.

They reached the horse and Ben said, "It is dead."

Riding around the animal, Dixie saw the ragged white diamond in its forehead and cried, "It's King's old lead mare."

Ben nodded grimly and said, "Yes."

"They ran her to death," Dixie cried, bitterness coming into her voice.

Ben dismounted and approached the mare, looking at a dark stain in the dry earth under her neck. "She didn't die from running," he said. "They shot her. Look at that. It's a bullet hole." He pointed to a round hole just in front of the mare's shoulder.

"But . . . but, why would they do that?" Dixie asked, bewildered.

"Because she was too smart to go into the trap," Ben said angrily. "She wouldn't go in, and the others wouldn't go in without her. So they shot her. They figured that next time, without her, they might get them in. They shot her."

Dixie sat looking at the lifeless form, then said, "What a dirty, rotten trick!"

CHAPTER ELEVEN

BEN AND Dixie Darby were stunned by their discovery of the dead mare in the brush. During the years that they had watched King's band they had come to know this wise old leader and to regard her with admiration and affection. In her way, she was as important to the welfare of the bunch as King himself. In times of danger and confusion, it was she who determined the instant to flee and who chose the direction. King kept watch and challenged all suspicious movements; he brought up the rear and drove the laggards. But the old mare was the leader, the field general who kept her eyes to the front. And the others followed her without question. Now she was dead. She had refused to lead the band into a trap, so they had shot her. They had shot her to increase the confusion and the desperation of the footsore, weary horses. It was hard for Ben and Dixie to understand such cruelty. Dixie was close to tears when Ben glanced up at her.

"Come on," Ben said, turning to his horse. "Let's get away from here, before I get any madder."

They rode through the sage, in the direction of Juniper Springs. "I hate this horse-running. I hate it!" Dixie said.

Ben did not reply. He was thinking, with a grim look on his face, and a few minutes later he reined his horse abruptly to the left.

"Where're you going?" Dixie asked.

"This way," Ben replied.

She did not question him further but followed.

Ben rode across to the mouth of the sink, entered it and rode between the rising walls. At the place where the poles were piled against the wall he reined up, regarded them for a minute and then went on. Presently they came to the lower fence. Ben pulled up and sat looking at it.

"Well," he said, as if surprised, "here's a fence. It's in our way. No gate. I guess we'd better make one."

He took down his rope, tossed the loop over one of the posts, and turned Inky against the rope. The post bent, cracked, then broke off at the ground. The rails held it upright, however. Ben took the loop from that post and put it on another one. This post cracked and broke also, and the section of rails between the two posts fell to the ground. Ben dismounted and threw the rails aside, then he got back on Inky and rode through the opening. "Come on," he said to Dixie.

"What did you do that for?" Dixie asked, as they were riding away.

"Because I wanted to get through," Ben said. "When a man puts a fence up on open range like this, he ought to put a gate in it."

"You think that Tom will try to put the wild bunch in there again?" she said, after a minute.

"I don't know what he'll do," Ben said. "A man who'll kill a good mare like that might do anything."

"He'll be madder than a wet hen," Dixie said.

"Let him be," Ben said.

They rode into Juniper Springs and watered their horses, then headed out across Fickle Flats. "We'll hit the Wolf Creek trail," Ben said.

This was a longer distance back to the ranch, but it was the shortest way out of the high country. Dixie knew that Ben was taking that route because he did not want to run the risk of being seen by some rider from the Basin Lake camp, who might be in the vicinity of Gailey Ridge or the Three Deck trail. Despite his anger, Ben was taking precautions, knowing that Tom Sample could make serious trouble for them.

They kept a careful watch for horsemen across Fickle Flats, but saw none, and after they dropped down into Wolf Creek breaks their vigilance relaxed and a nervous reaction took its place.

"Are you going to tell Pop?" Dixie asked, when they reached the well-defined trail down in Wolf Creek.

"No," Ben said. "What can he do?"

"It would make him pretty mad to know that Tom Sample is shooting horses," Dixie said.

"Yes, but there's nothing he can do about it. There's no law against shooting a wild horse."

"No, but he wouldn't like it," she insisted.

Ben shook his head. "It wouldn't help any. Now, if it . . ." He reined up suddenly and said, "Do you think they've shot any more?"

"I don't know," she said. "I wouldn't put anything past them."

Ben looked back up the creek and for a brief instant considered returning to the high country. "If they hurt Tanger," he said, "I'll . . . I'll . . ."

"They'd better not," Dixie said, her blue eyes flashing dangerously.

Ben touched his horse on along the trail. "Gee, it's awful, Dix, to shoot horses like that," he said.

"I'll bet Pearly Maunderland did it," she said. "He's the meanest one."

"Yes," Ben said. Pearly prided himself on being a good marksman. Ben remembered hearing him brag about the long range at which he had killed an antelope. And the day they had seen him after they had tried to cut Tanger out of the wild bunch there had been a rifle in his saddle boot. Pearly always seemed to have a gun handy, a fact which caused Ben to believe that at heart the man was really a coward. Cowardice and cruelty were usually closely akin.

Ben and Dixie were silent at the supper table that night, and Ben was glad his father did not ask them where they had been. It had been an irritating and disappointing day, without hope or encouragement, and Ben did not want to talk about it. And he could see no gain in annoying his father with the news of the dead mare. None of them could do anything about her now.

After supper, when they were in the living room alone, Dixie said, "Are you going back tomorrow?"

Ben shook his head. He would like to go, he would like to see how Tanger was getting along, but he knew that he could not do any good and he knew that tempers would be explosive up there now. Something unpleasant could happen, and Ben's better judgment told him to stay away.

His father did not have any particular job in mind for Ben the next day, so Ben cut wood, deliberately choosing a task that he did not like. The wood box by the kitchen range had been his first serious responsibility. It was one for which he still had a strong distaste. But on this day he sharpened the ax on the grindstone and went to work on the brittle limbs with grim-eyed purpose.

When he came back to the house at noon, his father noticed the pile that had been cut and broken into stove lengths and said, "What's the matter, Ben? Are you sick?"

"No sir," Ben said, resting his ax and grinning. "I just decided this was a good time to get a supply of wood cut up. Later on we'll be pretty busy, I expect."

"That's right. It's a good idea," Vince said, but as he went into the house he shook his head as if not certain he had heard correctly.

The woodpile kept Ben's hands busy but his mind kept straying up to the high country and it was a far from satisfactory day. Dixie kept close to the house, helping her mother with the ironing, and Ben knew she was unhappy too.

Ben was in no hurry to get up the next morning and he was the last to finish breakfast. He decided that he might as well do some riding, so he got his hat and started for the corrals. He would ride on Crystal Mountain, where most of Tack's cattle ranged at this time of the year and where, since he would be on the opposite side of the canyon, there would not be any temptation to stretch his ride to Bascomb Flats or Juniper Springs.

But while Ben was in the runway, saddling Inky, he heard an angry voice talking to his father. "I'm pretty sore, Vince," Tom Sample's voice said. "Here we've been after the mustangs three weeks and yesterday afternoon we put 'em in a trap, and somebody had cut our fence."

"Cut your fence?" Vince said.

"Yes. We rigged up a trap in a little canyon, put a fence across one end of it and got a bunch of poles and rails for the other end. We built it high enough so there wasn't a chance they could jump it, and three days ago it was all right. I looked it over myself to make sure. But late yesterday afternoon we turned the wild bunch in there, put every horse in the herd down between the walls. We would've had them, but when they hit the lower fence they went right on through it."

Inside the barn Ben's eyes grew round with concern. He knew he should have expected this, but up in Twin Buttes, after they had found the dead mare, he had been so angry he did not care. Now he knew a quick regret at his obstinate anger and suspected that he had weakened his position.

"You believe someone cut it?" Vince said.

"Broke the posts off," Tom said. "We found where they did it. They broke off two posts and pulled down the rails. It was wide open when the horses hit it. They hardly checked their speed going through."

"I see," Vince said, his voice slow and thoughtful. "You have any idea who did it?"

There was a slight hesitation, then Tom Sample said, "Yes," defiantly.

Ben heard the back door slam and, glancing through one of the windows, saw Dixie coming from the house, wearing levis and boots. He tried to wigwag a warning to her but, though he knew she must see him, she came on steadily.

The two men were standing near the horse corral, at the end of the runway. Looking along the stalls, Ben could see the rear half of Tom's horse.

"You got any proof who did it?" Vince said, with a ring in his voice.

Again Tom Sample hesitated, and then he said, "No, not actual proof. But I've got a pretty strong idea."

"What do you base it on?" Vince said.

"Well, Ben and Dixie have been riding up there, Vince. Pearly saw them one afternoon."

There was a short silence, and then Vince noticed Dixie, who had just arrived.

"Dixie, have you been riding in Twin Buttes?" he asked sharply.

Ben knew that hiding was useless. He took Inky's rein and walked out into the bright morning light.

"Here's Ben," Vince said, turning to him. "Ben, have you and Dixie been riding up in Twin Buttes?"

"Yes sir," Ben said.

"What were you doing up there?"

"We . . . we . . ."

"We were after Tanger," Dixie said. "We were trying to get him up."

"Tanger? Is Tanger up there?"

"Yes sir," Ben said.

"What's he doing up there?" Vince demanded.

"He's running with the wild bunch," Tom Sample said. "We've seen him a couple of times."

"He was up in the head of Fickle Creek and he strayed up on the flats," Ben said. "I tracked him. He took up with a wild band up there."

"Hasn't he got sense enough to stay at home?" Vince said.

"He didn't know he was doing anything wrong," Ben said. "He just happened to be up where he could see the wild horses when they came along."

"He acts like he's gone wild," Tom said.

"He has not," Ben said quickly.

"We tried to cut him out a couple of times, but he was too wild for us," Tom said.

[138]

"We asked Pearly to let us cut him out, and he wouldn't do it," Dixie said.

"You wanted to scatter the bunch," Tom said. "Pearly told me about it."

"All we wanted was Tanger," Dixie said. "He's Ben's horse and he's branded."

"We can't help it because he's in the wild bunch," Tom said to Vince. "We didn't put him there."

"No," Vince had to admit.

"When we catch them, we'll put a rope on him and bring him down for you," Tom said, eager to seem helpful.

"Don't," Ben said. "Don't even touch him."

Tom acted surprised. "All right, if that's what you want. I thought we would save you some riding."

"You should know that's what I want," Ben said. "I told Pearly not to touch him."

"We wouldn't hurt him."

"I'm not so sure of that," Dixie said.

Tom shrugged and said, "All I came down for was to find out who cut my fence." He eyed Ben sharply.

"Yes," Vince said, "I wanted to ask you about that, Ben."

"I did it," Ben said.

Vince's eyes widened with displeasure. "You did? Why?"

"I was riding through the canyon," Ben said, "and I came to the fence. It wasn't holding anything and . . . and it was in my way. There weren't any horses."

"But you knew I had put it there for a trap," Tom said

accusingly. "You could see that it had just been repaired. You knew we planned to run the mustangs in there."

"They're not mustangs," Dixie said. "They're good horses."

"Whatever they are, Ben knew we figured to catch them in there," Tom said.

"Couldn't you have gone around the fence, Ben?" his father asked.

"Yes sir," Ben said.

"Then why didn't you?"

"I . . . I didn't want to."

"That's not the real reason we cut it," Dixie declared. "The real reason was the dead mare."

"Dead mare?" Vince repeated.

"What dead mare?" Tom Sample said.

"You know what dead mare," Dixie said. "She was a swell horse," she went on, turning to her father. "She was the leader of King's band; she was always out in front."

"She was smart too," Ben said. "That's the reason they killed her."

"Killed her?" Vince frowned.

"Who killed her?" Tom said.

"You did," Dixie said. "Or one of your men did. It's the same thing."

"I haven't killed any horse," Tom said.

"You found her?" Vince said.

"Yes, she was out in the brush," Ben said.

"What makes you think she was killed?" Vince said.

"There was a bullet hole through her neck," Dixie declared.

"Bullet hole? You sure?"

"Yes sir," Ben said. "I looked at it. She was running when it knocked her down. She bled a lot on the ground."

Vince turned to Tom. "What about that, Tom?" he said, his voice hard.

"I didn't do it," Tom said.

"They did it because she wouldn't lead the band into the trap," Dixie said. "It was the same place where Tom caught them two years ago and she still remembered it. She wouldn't go in again."

"She was just a broomtail, Vince," Tom said. "It's done all the time, you know that. That's about the only way to get rid of some of these knot-headed stallions."

"I don't like shooting horses," Vince said, his big voice booming.

"There's no law against it," Tom said.

"I still don't like it," Vince repeated.

Tom was irritated at finding himself on the defensive. Obviously he had not known that Ben and Dixie had found the dead mare. "Well," he said, "I told you I didn't do it."

"Someone did," Dixie said. "Someone who is trying to catch King and his band did it. Who do you suppose that could be?"

"That'll do, Dix," her father said to her sternly, but it was easy to see that he was more displeased with Tom Sample. "Tell your men, Tom, to be mighty certain they

[141]

never put their sights on a horse of mine. There is a law against killing branded horses."

"You know I'm not going to bother any of your horses, Vince," Tom said. "I never have. But it's not right for Ben and Dixie to cut my fence, either."

Vince paused. "No, that's true," he said. He turned to Ben. "Ben, you and Dix get on your horses and go up to Twin Buttes and fix that fence. Put it back just the way you found it. And when you've finished, come on back to the ranch. And in the future stay away from Twin Buttes. Don't ride up there for any reason, unless you talk it over with me first."

"That don't put the horses back," Tom pointed out unpleasantly. "We had 'em caught. We would have ropes on most of them by now."

Vince had to admit the truth of that and after a few seconds of serious thought he said, "I guess you're due something there. I can have Ben and Dixie help you catch them again, if that's what you want?"

The idea jolted Ben cruelly. His father couldn't mean that; he wouldn't make them help Tom Sample catch King! But he did mean it, and a look at his serious face was all Ben needed to know it.

Tom Sample was also surprised by the offer. At first he was inclined to reject it; but, after some quick and cunning consideration, he said, "Ben knows the stallion pretty well, Vince. He can help us, if you're of a mind to have him do it."

"I know him as well as Ben does," Dixie said quickly. "I helped catch him the other time."

Tom shook his head. "A horse-runners' camp is no place for a girl," he said.

"She can ride back and forth," Vince said. "That's what I intended."

But Tom knew Dixie's sharp fiery little temper and he said, "It's too far, Vince. Ben can put up at Basin Lake with us. It ought not to take but a few more days."

Ben still could hardly believe it. He knew that because of him Tom had not caught the horses; he had been wrong in breaking down the fence, but the possibility that his father might, because of his strong sense of justice, require him to help catch the stallion had not occurred to him. His father knew, of course, that Ben had been fervently hoping for days that Tom Sample would not be successful.

Vince Darby said, "Get your bedroll, Ben. You can take Buck along for an extra horse."

CHAPTER TWELVE

Riding behind Tom Sample up Three Deck trail that warm summer morning, Ben pondered unhappily on the strange set of circumstances that had made him the assistant of a man for whom he had no respect, in an undertaking which he wholeheartedly hoped would fail. He did not like Tom Sample and he did not want King to be captured, but he found himself in the position of being duty bound to give Tom all the assistance he could. His father had not given him explicit instructions as to that, but Ben knew that it had been understood. His father would never have sent him up there had he not felt strongly about the matter, and there was no question in Ben's mind as to what Pop intended.

The fault, of course, went back to Ben's act in cutting the canyon fence. He had known that it was wrong, that he had no right to do it, but he had been so irritated by the shooting of the old lead mare that, at the time, he had not cared. It was too late now to be sorry. So the only thing that he could do was to try to make amends in line with his father's decision, and that would not be easy. It would be galling to have to ride for Tom Sample, and it would be torture to have to assist in capturing the black stallion.

Ben let his eyes come up to Tom Sample's straight narrow back. Tom had been silent since they left the ranch and Ben wondered what was going on in the horse-runner's mind. Tom, Ben believed, had been surprised by his father's offer, and Ben wondered why Tom had ever accepted it. Heretofore, Tom had made it plain that he did not want Ben up in Twin Buttes while he was running horses; he had even warned him, as Pearly Maunderland had warned both Ben and Dixie, to stay away. But now Tom was accepting Ben as a rider and taking him to the Basin Lake camp. Ben thought he knew what had caused Tom to change his mind. Heretofore, Tom had been worried about Ben's interfering with the horse-running, as Ben of course had done in cutting the fence. Now Tom knew that Ben was bound by his father's commitment of assistance. He knew that the bond of loyalty and respect between the Darbys was strong. Ben could not prove faithless to his father's desire to be fair. Ben knew it, and he knew that Tom Sample knew it. But Ben did not blame his father; he knew he had brought it on himself.

"Where do you figure the wild bunch is now, Tom?" Ben asked. If he had to help catch the stallion, he decided that he might as well get about it, for the sooner the task was completed the quicker he could leave Tom Sample and go back to Tack.

"Standing Rock," Tom said, without turning. "Amos

Boskins picked them up this morning. Dick Crow will relieve him at noon."

"They should be pretty well run down," Ben said.

"They are. We ought to have had them before now."

"Did you ever consider separating the stallion from the rest of the bunch? That's the way I caught him before. Without the others, he loses some of his fight."

"What good would that do?" Tom said. "I want to catch the works. I might as well take the best colts and young mares. I figure to put them in that trap."

Ben saw Tom's reasoning in that statement, although he hated to see the colts leave the high country. But it was his job to help and he said, "I know where there's another trap, one better than that."

"Where?"

"On the north slope of Gailey. It's a canyon that runs back into the ridge. The mouth is pretty wide but the walls close in up aways, and one man can fix the upper end in half a day."

"You think they'll go in it?" Tom asked with interest.

"They'll go in," Ben said. "I've seen them in there feeding. There's grass enough for a month."

"We'll look at it," Tom said. "But the place we've got is not bad."

Ben remembered something then and he said, "I guess I'd better ride over and fix that fence."

"You're sorry now you busted it down, aren't you?" Tom said, turning in his saddle.

Ben did not like the smile on the man's face and had a

quick impulse to say no, emphatically. He quickly realized however that this would merely add to his difficulties,
so he evaded an answer by saying, "I'll swing over and fix
it up."

"Want me to take Buck on in?" Tom offered.

"No, he won't be any trouble," Ben said. He did not
want to turn the horse over to Tom. "As soon as I finish,
I'll come on to Basin Lake."

Tom nodded. "I told Pearly to fix it this morning, but
you can ride over and take a look. If he's not finished, you
can help him. There's some tools at the upper end."

Ben was glad to get away from Tom, for he felt that
the man was getting a malicious satisfaction out of the
situation. But if he had suspected that Pearly Maunderland would be at the the canyon, he would have been reluctant to make the offer to fix the fence because, of the two,
he preferred Tom.

Pearly was there. Ben, as he rode up along the canyon
floor, could see that the man had not made much progress.
He had one post reset and was digging a hole for the other
one. His horse whinnied and he looked up, frowning when
he saw who was coming.

"What're you doing here?" Pearly said sourly. His eyes
were red rimmed from riding in the dust and the thick
stubble of beard on his square jaw was black. "I thought I
told you to stay away."

Ben had been dreading this. "I'm helping Tom now,"
he said. "I came over to help you."

"What?" Pearly said, disbelieving.

Ben nodded his head. "I'm going to help Tom catch the black stallion," he said. "I rode over to help you put this fence up."

"But . . . but you tore it down," Pearly said.

"Yes," Ben said unhappily. "That's the reason I'm here."

"Something's wrong about this," Pearly said.

"No it's not. Pop said, because it was my fault that the bunch got away yesterday, I had to help Tom catch them again. That's the way Pop figures it. I came up from the ranch with Tom. He headed on in to Basin Lake. He told me I might find you here."

Maunderland's little eyes studied Ben, then went on to the buckskin horse with its bedroll pack, and presently the frown on his face was replaced by a grin. "Well, I'll be darned!" he said. "So you're riding for Tom? You're going to help us catch the black stallion?"

"Yes," Ben said weakly.

"Well, well, that's fine. That's just dandy. You can start right in by fixin' this fence you broke down."

"All right," Ben said. He dismounted and loosened his saddle cinch. Then he went to Buck to loosen the pack cinch.

"Never mind about that," Pearly said. "This post-hole digger is waitin' for you."

"All right," Ben said, but he loosened the cinch anyway.

Pearly handed him the digger and said, "Right there. Put it down good and deep."

Ben punched the digger into the shallow hole until

some dirt was loose, then lifted the dirt out. Pearly stood and watched him. Ben kept digging. After a few minutes, Pearly, with the sly grin still on his face, went along the fence to a shady spot and sat down. Ben worked steadily and soon the sweat was appearing through his blue shirt.

"That's deep enough," Pearly said. "Now set the post. There it is."

Ben went to his horse, took his canteen from the saddle and had a drink first. "You want a drink?" he asked.

"No," Pearly said, scowling.

Ben went back to his work. He set the post, tamped it in, feeling that Pearly was taking undue advantage of the situation.

"Okay, now put up the rails," Pearly said. "Wire 'em good and tight, like they were before you broke 'em down."

Two persons could have handled the rails with twice the speed and ease, but Pearly did not help Ben. He sat in the shade and watched, with a critical look on his face. Ben put up one end of a rail, wired it, then went to the other end and raised and wired it. It was slow, but rail by rail the fence came up and the gap closed. Noon came and passed. Ben had no lunch and Pearly said nothing about eating. The sun beat down into the little canyon and sweat trickled down across Ben's face. At last the top rail was up and fastened in place. Ben stepped back and looked at the fence, first at the repaired section and then along its whole length.

Maunderland got up, tested one of the rails with a strong pull. "That'll hold them," he said.

Ben had his eye on another place. "It could be a little higher there," he said. He searched around until he found another rail and fastened it in the low place. Some ends of wire had been left sticking out and Ben got a stone and beat them down flat, so they would not pierce or cut a horse's hide.

Pearly went along the fence, testing its strength at various spots.

"That's good enough," he said. "Let's get going." He became moodily silent as they rode through the brush.

Tom Sample was at Basin Lake when Ben and Pearly arrived. Saddle horses were feeding on the grassy flat and Ben pulled the rigging from Inky and Buck and turned them loose. He put his saddles under a bush and carried his bedroll into the grove of trees to the camp. Tom Sample said, "Well, did you get it fixed?"

"Yes," Ben said.

"We'll be all right," Pearly said, "if somebody don't break it down again."

Ben knew the jibe was aimed at him, but he let it pass. He glanced around and saw only two bedrolls. "Where's the other camp?" he asked Tom.

"Little Butte," Tom said.

Ben nodded. Little Butte water hole was on the other side of the circle and two men, working from there, could keep the horses moving through Standing Rock and the country north of Gailey Ridge. Divided camps cut down the necessary riding.

Ben was hungry. He gathered some wood and made a

fire on the old ashes. "Grub's in the alforjas," Tom said. "There's a pot of beans you can warm up."

Ben cooked the supper, which consisted of beans, bacon, potatoes, and bread. He made a big pot of black coffee. "Come and get it," he said. He filled his own plate and began to eat.

"You're pretty handy to have around," Tom said.

Tom and Pearly sat and talked, but as soon as Ben had finished with the dishes he spread his bedroll and turned in, selecting a place well away from the fire. He had no desire to listen to the two men. He had to work for Tom Sample, but he did not feel that he had to pretend to like the job. He tried to keep his thoughts away from the black stallion and his band, but it was long after the stars were bright in the wide dark sky before he went to sleep.

Ben was the first one up the next morning. He cooked breakfast and ate, leaving food for Tom and Pearly in pans near the coals. Both of them were still in their beds. Ben went past the little lake and out to the meadow to look at his horses. He caught Inky first and checked his feet to make certain the shoes were all tight. Then he looked at Buck. They were both all right. Ben went to his pack, got out the two nose bags and put a little grain in each of them from the small sack he had brought from the ranch. When he put these bags on Inky and Buck, the other horses crowded around, and Ben noticed that they were thin. The strain was beginning to tell even on Tom's saddle horses. While Inky and Buck ate, Ben checked his saddle, the cinch and stirrup leathers, and looked over his rope. He knew his equipment was all right, but it gave him something to do.

Tom Sample came down to the lake and washed his face and hands. A little later Pearly came and washed. Ben took the nose bags from his horses and carried them, with the grain, back to the trees. He knew that if he left the grain, the other horses, aware that it was there, would tear the sack and scatter it.

"What do you want me to do, Tom?" Ben said.

"About noon you can go up and pick the bunch up and bring it on down here," Tom said.

"And keep 'em moving," Pearly said pointedly.

Ben said to Tom, "Do you want to take a look at that other canyon I was telling you about? It's on this side of Gailey."

"No," Tom said.

"They'll go in there," Ben said.

"They'll go in the one we've got ready," Pearly said.

"Maybe," Ben said.

"You'll see," Pearly said.

Ben sighted the dust early in the afternoon. He swung wide to get behind the horses. The other rider, back half a mile or so, saw Ben and waved his hat. Ben waved in reply and the rider turned back, heading for the Little Butte Creek camp.

Ben turned after the wild horses and touched Buck to an easy gallop. He could see a dark form moving in the dust and knew it was King. But there was no proud whinny and challenge as in the past. King was traveling at a slow trot and Buck's gallop cut down the distance between them. Presently Ben was close enough to see that the big black horse was thin and dust caked. Ben was within a hundred yards before King broke into a gallop, and the heavy pounding action had little resemblance to the swift easy flight that Ben remembered.

Ben felt a quick pang of pity. The long days of relentless running had sapped King's strength until he no longer looked or acted like the same horse. Ben touched Buck to a slightly faster gallop, and a second or two later King matched the faster gait. There was an increase of dust up in front. But King did not try to pull away. Days of running had taught him that he could not elude the horsemen. Ben slacked his pace to a jog and immediately King slowed down too. The dust lessened and Ben could see the other horses, plodding wearily in front of the stallion. The weak horses and colts had dropped out days before and these were the best of the band.

It was after dark when the wild horses moved past Basin Lake. Ben turned Buck in, stripped off his gear at the edge of the grove and watched while Buck went to the water and drank. Ben washed his face and hands to get rid of the accumulated dust, then went through the trees to the camp. Coals of a recent fire glowed in the ashes.

"Your grub's in the pan," Tom Sample said. Tom was sitting lazily on a kitchen box. Pearly Maunderland had his back to a tree.

Ben took the pan, got a knife and fork, and began to eat. "Where'd you leave them?" Tom said presently.

"Back there," Ben said, jerking his head.

"It took you long enough," Pearly said. "Can't that buckskin take it?"

"I kept them moving," Ben said.

"You pick them up in the morning at daylight, Pearly," Tom said.

"Better let me get the black," Pearly said. "The others'll be easy after that."

"No," Tom said, "We'll take them all together."

The feeling that had been damming up inside Ben all afternoon broke loose. "Well, it's time you did it," he said hotly. "What're you trying to do, kill them on their feet? They're so tired and sore footed they can hardly walk."

"That's just the way I want them," Tom said. "This time there's not going to be any slip-up."

"A few more days of this, and there won't be any horses," Ben said. "You can catch them with ropes in the morning."

"That's all you know about it," Pearly said. "There's a lot of fight left in that stud yet."

"There'll always be a lot of fight in him," Ben said. "But there's no use in killing off the rest of them, too." He did not try to keep the anger and scorn out of his voice.

"I'm running this outfit," Tom reminded him testily.

"I'm glad I'm not," Ben said. "I wouldn't want it on my conscience."

"You're taking orders from me," Tom said, "or you can go back to Tack and tell Vince you wouldn't work." Tom's temper was up.

Ben considered this a few seconds, then said, "I'm taking orders."

"That's better," Tom said.

"And don't try any tricks," Pearly said.

Ben threw the rest of his food to the ground and went to his bedroll, not trusting himself to engage in the bickering any longer. He would do what he had to, he told himself, but not one turn more. He was sick of the whole business.

Pearly Maunderland was up before daylight, cooked a quick breakfast, caught a horse, and rode away. Ben heard the drum of his horse's feet through the hard, dry ground. He listened till it faded away, then turned over and tried to go back to sleep.

The sun was up when Tom Sample rekindled the fire. Ben got up and helped with the breakfast. Neither of them spoke, and Ben knew Tom had not forgot their argument of the previous night.

The tension did not lessen and about the middle of the morning Tom got his hat and said, "You stay in camp today, Ben. Stay here and keep watch on things."

"All right," Ben said.

"Till I get back," Tom said, and turned and left the grove on his stocking-footed horse.

Ben had a miserable day, doing nothing. He went over his equipment again, and cleaned up the camp, burning the trash and rubbish that had accumulated. But this took only a few hours. Ben's restlessness increased. Something was happening out there in the brush, something Tom and Pearly had not talked about. Ben was certain that it was a drive to catch the wild horses but, whatever it was, Tom Sample very plainly did not want Ben around.

It was a long, irksome day but Ben obeyed Tom Sample to the letter, despite a consuming curiosity to know what was going on in the brush. Late in the afternoon he made a big fire of juniper limbs, tended it carefully until it was a bed of glowing coals. He found a can of blueberries in one of the kitchen boxes and made a thick juicy pie, baking it in a dutch oven. He sliced bacon and onions into a big kettle of beans and put it on to boil.

It was after sundown when Ben heard horses in the meadow. He set the dutch oven with the newly mixed biscuits on the coals and put on the hot lid. The coffeepot was filled with fresh water and Ben raised the top and dumped in the coffee. If they wanted him to be the cook, as seemed obvious, he would be a good one.

Through the trees Ben could see four men unsaddling horses, and he knew that the other two riders had come in from Little Butte camp. One by one, as they finished, they came to the camp. Ben needed only one look at their dust-caked faces to know that whatever they had attempted that day had not been successful.

"It's ready, when you are," Ben told Tom.

They took towels from the limbs of the trees and went to the lake to wash. Ben could hear them snorting and blowing. Soon they were back. The dust was gone from their tanned bearded faces but the scowls and disappointment were still there. As Ben spooned the food into the tin plates, he was aware of an unpleasant tension in the air. Ben knew that they did not catch the horses, but he did not know whether he was pleased or sorry. This thing had to end. The wild horses could not take much more, and neither could he.

"I'll get him," Pearly Maunderland blurted angrily. "I'll get him tomorrow."

None of the three men answered and Pearly glared around at them.

"What happened today?" Ben asked.

"That's none of your business," Pearly snarled.

Ben shrugged his shoulders, signifying his willingness to let the matter drop.

But Pearly would not have it that way. "You think you're mighty smart, don't you?" he said. "If it hadn't been for you, we'd have had them now. I've a good notion to kick you out of camp."

The man was in such a temper that Ben decided it was best not to reply.

"You're the cause of all our trouble," Pearly went on. "It would serve you right if I kicked you out of camp."

Ben had enough. "I might leave, if Tom tells me to," he said. "But you won't kick me."

"Is that so?" Pearly said, getting to his feet. "I should have given you a good licking the first time I caught you up here. Then you wouldn't have cut the fence."

Ben was erect now and alert. He knew he would be no match for the man and did not believe Pearly would dare attack him. But he had no intention of permitting Pearly to touch him.

"Aw, forget it," one of the riders said disgustedly.

"You shut up," Pearly said to him.

Just then there was a sound of horses in the meadow and Tom Sample said, "What's that?"

They all listened. One of the feeding horses neighed and was answered.

"Someone's coming," one of the riders said.

Pearly Maunderland grumbled under his breath, sat back down again, and picked up his plate. The sound of hoofs came on and dark forms dismounted at the edge of the grove. A man came into the circle of the firelight. Ben's jaw dropped with amazement. The man was Andy Blair. And close behind him came Vince, and close behind him was Dixie. Ben felt so relieved he could have cried.

CHAPTER THIRTEEN

Tom Sample's amazement, when he saw who the newcomer was, equaled Ben's, but he recovered quickly and jumped to his feet. "Hello, Mr. Blair," he cried. "Well, of all people! And at this time of the night? You're just in time for supper. Here, Ben, get Mr. Blair a plate—and one for your pop and Dixie, too."

"Hello, Tom," Blair said, glancing around the camp. He nodded at Pearly and the other two men. "Hello, Ben. How's it going?"

"All right," Ben said. He began to scurry about, finding plates and putting food on them. Dixie came to the fire and squatted on her heels to help.

"Ben's been helping us with the cooking," Tom Sample said, his voice friendly and cheerful. "He's one of the best camp cooks I ever ate after. Tonight he made a pie that'll melt in your mouth. We're just finishing; we were late getting in."

Andy Blair accepted a plate from Dixie and said, "Thanks. That looks good."

"I didn't look for you back for a week yet," Tom said. "Here, Vince, sit here. I figured to have Midnight Chief all tied up and ready for you by the time you got back."

"Then you haven't caught him yet?" Blair said.

"No. He's been giving us a pretty good run. He's just a lot of horse, Mr. Blair. I'll bet old Midnight Fire couldn't do any better. You certainly are going to have a wonderful horse. No doubt about that."

"It's taking you a long time," Blair said.

"Yes," Tom said. "We've been taking it pretty easy with him. But we'll get him. As a matter of fact, we've practically got him now. Almost did today. I wouldn't be surprised in the least if we got him tomorrow. Would you, Pearly?"

"No," Pearly said.

Andy Blair shook his head. "You won't get him, Tom," he said. "You're through running him."

Tom blinked his eyes. "But . . . but we haven't caught him yet. You hired us to catch him."

"Yes, I did," Blair said. "But now I'm firing you. Figure your time and I'll pay you off."

"But . . . why?" Tom was plainly perturbed.

"I won't have a man working for me who shoots horses," Andy Blair said.

Tom's eyes widened. "Shoots horses?" He looked toward Pearly Maunderland briefly.

"That's what I said. I've worked with horses all my life but I've never shot one yet or permitted anyone else to, unless they had to be destroyed for some humane reason."

"But . . . but . . ." Tom gave Ben a disgusted look.

[160]

He knew, however, that there was no use in denying it. "This was just a range broomtail. She wasn't worth the powder it took."

"She was," Dixie said sharply. "She was King's old lead mare. She was a fine old mare and plenty smart."

"That was the trouble," Tom said, explaining to Andy Blair. "She was too smart. We had a trap built and she wouldn't go into it. And the rest wouldn't go until she did. Can't you see, we had to get her out of the way in order to catch Midnight Chief for you."

"We would have had him now, and the others too, if Ben hadn't broke down our fence," Pearly said bitterly.

"Yes, I guess that's right," Ben admitted to Andy Blair.

"That's the reason I sent Ben up here to help," Vince said. "He shouldn't have done it."

"Blame him, not us," Tom Sample said, in a righteous tone.

Ben's feeling of guilt was stronger than ever.

"I'm not blaming anyone," Blair said, "because the stallion has not been caught. But I will not have anyone working for me who deliberately shoots down an uninjured horse. That's final. Give me your bill, Tom, and in the morning pack your horses and take your riders and get out of here."

"But you want your stallion, don't you?" Tom cried.

"Not the way you catch horses," Blair said. "I'm paying you off tonight, just as soon as we can figure up what I owe you."

"You can't stop us from running horses up here," Pearly

Maunderland said angrily. "This is open range. We can run horses up here all we want and nobody can stop us."

"You can't run that black stallion," Andy Blair said firmly. "He's not a wild horse."

"Nor that chestnut gelding," Vince Darby said. "Not any more."

"They're both wearing brands," Dixie said gleefully.

"They're running with wild horses," Pearly Maunderland said in a surly manner. "Can we help it if they happen to be in the wild bunch we want?"

"It's not fair," Tom Sample said to Blair. "Here we've spent all this time up here, trying to catch a horse for you and, just when we've got them run down and ready to put ropes on, you fire us. That's not fair."

"I'll pay you," Blair said. "I'll pay you for all the time you've put in. That's all I ever said I'd do."

"But what about the other horses we were going to catch? There're some good colts there."

"That wasn't a part of my bargain," Blair said.

"We can keep running them," Pearly Maunderland said. "There's nothing to keep us from going on."

"But not on my payroll," Blair said.

"And not," Vince Darby said firmly, "until we've had a reasonable time to cut a couple of branded horses out of the bunch."

"There's no law that makes us do that," Pearly said.

"No, that's right," Vince said. "And there's no law that requires us to leave them in there, either."

"You can't interfere with us," Pearly said.

"I don't intend to," Vince said. "I'm just going to get a couple of horses wearing my brand."

"You're going after that stallion, that's what you're going to do," Tom said accusingly.

"Maybe," Vince said. "But I haven't agreed to yet."

"Well, you won't get him. I can tell you that," Pearly Maunderland said. He turned to Andy Blair and continued, "If you don't let us catch him, you'll never get him. If you want your horse, you had better let us go ahead."

"No," Blair said.

"He won't be much trouble to catch," Ben told Mr. Blair. "He's so sore footed now he can hardly walk. I don't know how they missed him today."

"I can tell you why," Tom said. "That blamed gelding was leading them and he wouldn't go into the trap."

"Tanger?" Dixie cried, not trying to conceal the delight in her voice.

"Yes."

"I can catch Tanger, Mr. Blair," Ben said eagerly. "He'll be easy to catch. And I'll . . . I'll catch the stallion for you. I'll catch him. I had him once and I can get him again."

"I thought perhaps you would, Ben," the man said.

"Yes sir," Ben said, gulping with the full realization of what he was promising to do. It would mean the end of his last hope, but anything was better than having Tom and Pearly run the big horse. "I'll get him for you."

Pearly Maunderland snorted scornfully. "You haven't got a chance," he said.

[163]

"Pop'll let the gaucho help me—won't you, Pop? And Dixie? That's all I'll need. We caught him before."

Vince grumbled a little under his breath but jerked his head.

"We'll get him and it shouldn't take long," Ben went on. "He's run down now and I know just how to do it."

"Ha, ha," Pearly Maunderland said mirthlessly.

"Are you sure you want to do this, Ben?" his father asked. "You're talking about King, you know."

Ben considered briefly and said, "Yes. He's run down to the bone now. I don't want Tom to run him any more—not ever."

"That's the only way to get him," Tom said. "You can't catch a wild horse without running him."

"You don't have to run him to death," Ben replied heatedly.

"Let's get together on your bill, Tom," Andy Blair said. "I want to pay you off."

"And there's something I want to know," Vince Darby said. "Do you figure to keep running horses up here on your own?"

"Why?" Tom said. "What difference does it make? They're wild horses."

"It makes this difference," Vince said. "I aim to get those two Tack horses out of the bunch, and if you figure to keep running I'll do it just as quick as I can, in order to get out of your way. A couple of days ought to be enough."

"I don't know," Tom said, after a second's thought. "I haven't decided yet."

"Now's a good time to make up your mind," Vince said.

"I'll have to talk to my boys first," Tom objected.

"Talk to them now. I'll wait."

"Okay," Tom said. He nodded his head to his riders and moved off into the darkness under the trees. The three men followed him and they went out of the grove.

"Might as well get this settled," Vince said to Andy Blair.

"Now's the time," Blair agreed.

"They'll keep running them," Ben said. "Even if Tom didn't want those colts, they'd do it just for spite. They'll cause us all the trouble they can."

"That's up to them," Vince said.

"All I want is my stallion," Andy Blair said.

"Two days' time ought to do it," Vince said. "One day to get up here and another one to get the job done. Where'll they be tomorrow, Ben?"

"In Standing Rock. We can hit them at Little Butte. I don't know about King though; he'll put up a fight."

"If we must," Vince said, "we'll drive him all the way to Tack. It ought not to be too hard, if we leave Tanger running loose with him."

"That might do it," Ben said. "He knows Tanger now. We can put Dixie out in front and Tanger will follow right into a corral."

They heard footsteps coming back through the trees and became silent. Tom Sample came into the light of the fire, his face set and bitter. "You can pay us off, Mr. Blair," he said. "He's your horse and your chase."

[165]

"You're leaving?" Ben cried, hopefully yet hardly believing.

Tom nodded. "We're short on grub and out of horse feed. We've decided to call it quits—for this time."

Andy Blair got out his checkbook and fountain pen.

"Get your horses and load your gear, Ben," Vince said. "We'll go down to Tack and come back tomorrow with some equipment and spare horses."

Ben tossed the few articles that belonged to him into his bed and rolled it. He put the pack on his shoulder and went out to catch his horses. By the time he had them saddled and his pack on Buck, his father and Andy Blair and Dixie were mounting at the edge of the grove. Ben angled across the meadow to them. Vince led the way out of the basin and into the rolling brush.

After a time Ben pushed his horse up beside his father's and said, "Pop, I've got a bedroll and a spare horse. There's no need of my going back to Tack tonight. I can cut across to Juniper Springs and sleep there. Then I can check the band in Standing Rock in the morning and meet you in the afternoon at Little Butte. What do you think about that?"

Vince considered it a minute, then said, "It sounds all right, but you haven't got any grub."

"Don't worry about that," Ben said. "I had a big supper. I can wait till tomorrow."

Dixie fumbled at the back of her saddle and said, "Here're some sandwiches I brought along—just in case."

"You would," Ben said to her, grinning. He took the package and tied it on his own saddle.

[166]

"You sure you'll be all right?" Andy Blair asked.

"Sure," Ben answered. "I'll see you at Little Butte tomorrow."

"Don't try to put a rope on that black stallion by yourself," Vince warned seriously. "He's liable to be more than you can handle."

"I won't," Ben promised. "Gee, Mr. Blair," he went on, "it was sure a lucky thing you got here."

"It wasn't all luck," Andy Blair said. "I got on a plane just as soon as I received your father's telegram."

"What telegram?" Ben asked.

"The one telling me that Tom Sample's riders were shooting horses," Andy Blair said.

CHAPTER FOURTEEN

STARS WERE flung across the blue-black night like tiny pieces of a broken light. A soft breeze curled and eddied over the broken ground, stirring afresh the bowls that held the scent of the sage. The soft plopping of the horses' feet on the dusty earth was broken by the occasional ring of iron against stone.

A herd of antelope flushed from Juniper Springs as Ben rode in. He could see their ghostlike movements and hear the drum of their small hoofs. The water hole was low. The dryness, with its dust and baked earth, was one of the reasons the wild horses had suffered so much during the running.

Ben unsaddled and turned his horses loose, putting light hobbles on them as a precaution. He had no desire to wake up in the morning and find that, as gentle as they were, they had been stampeded into a wild bunch that had come in during the night for water. He unrolled his bed on a little rise that caught the breeze, undressed, and lay listening to the small sounds of the night. He marveled at the difference a few hours could make in one's outlook on life. Back in Tom Sample's camp everything had been so hopeless and bitter; now he was free. He realized then that his father had planned this. His father knew that his telegram would bring Andy Blair in a hurry. Even though for a while it had seemed so, his father had not been unmindful of Ben.

He was happy that Tom Sample and his riders were leaving the high country, that—for the time being—they were through running the wild horses. But his happiness was mixed with a deep sadness, for he knew that the black stallion was lost to the high country. There was no longer any hope that King could remain. He himself, and his father too, were pledged to deliver the horse to Andy Blair. They would catch King, help Andy Blair load him into a trailer, and wave good-by as Andy set out for Arizona. The matter was settled now. But Ben, though he liked Andy Blair and knew King would have a good home, could not be happy about the matter. He somehow knew that King, if it were possible for him to have a knowing choice, would prefer to live out his existence as a free wild stallion, guarding his mares and enduring the storms and the cold winters, till in the natural course of events he fell beneath a younger stallion's hoofs or the cunning leap of a cougar. That was the way King had lived and that was the way he should die. Ben knew the big horse would never be content in a box stall. But they had given their word. Ben turned over and tried to concentrate on going to sleep.

He ate two of Dixie's three sandwiches the next morning, filled his canteen, and rode east, into the Standing

Rock country. As he rode he kept a sharp outlook for horses. He guessed that Tom Sample and his riders had tried to put the band in the canyon trap the previous evening and had quit soon after they realized that the attempt was useless. The sorefooted horses would not have traveled far after that.

Ben rode to the canyon in which the trap had been fixed, and at the north end of it there was a great mass of fresh but confused sign. Tracks whirled and turned in all directions and Ben knew that it was here that the wild bunch, suspicious in that uncanny way horses know things, had broken back against the pursuers and scattered. Ben knew there had been some wild riding and shouting, and swinging of ropes, but in the end the wild horses had won, led by the smart Tanger who had no terror of rope-swinging horsemen. Probably because of his better physical condition, he had assumed the vacant place of leadership left by the death of the old mare. Ben was amazed at Tanger, and proud of him too. It was not often that geldings held any place of importance in a wild band.

Ben headed into Standing Rock. A little later, among the hoof tracks, his eye caught a flash of color and he swung down. It was a rifle cartridge, the primer dented and the bullet gone. It had not been there long and Ben deduced that it was the cartridge used to kill the bay mare.

Ben followed the line of sign leading into Standing Rock and had progressed a couple of miles when he saw a lone horse on a little rise in the brush. It raised its head and whinnied, not a challenge but a call mixed of friend-liness and suspicion. At first Ben supposed it was one of the mares that had dropped out of the running and that her colt was lying somewhere near. But as he watched, an-other horse got to its feet, and another one and still a third. Ben turned Inky toward them. The first horse whinnied again and came a short distance in Ben's direction. It was a chestnut.

"Tanger!" Ben said. "Tanger, you old rascal."

He began to whistle and call, riding toward Tanger all the while. Other horses began to appear over the brush as they got to their feet, and Ben knew this was the band. But something was wrong. Something was missing. King? King should have been the one to see him first instead of Tanger. Before now the black stallion should have been out to challenge him. Footsore and weary himself, King was probably lying down. The horses continued to get up until there was nearly a score of them, but still King did not appear. Ben could not understand it. He rode on. The horses bunched nervously and started to move away. Tanger, despite Ben's calling, moved around in front of them and they went off at a jog trot. Now of course King would appear; King always brought up the rear, where he could keep track of everything that was going on. But the stallion was not to be seen. The band traveled half a mile, and still no King.

Ben reined up, a puzzled frown on his face. Obviously King was not with the band. In fact, as far as Ben could determine, there was not any stallion with it, which was something Ben, in all his years of watching the wild horses, had never seen before.

Ben looked all around in the bed area. He saw an abundance of hoof sign and the smooth-pressed places where the horses had lain. He rode about, half afraid he might come on the black, injured or dead from exhaustion. The strain of running on a stallion was heavy because of the responsibility he assumed for the others. But Ben remembered that, when he had last seen King, the big horse, though thin, had seemed to have plenty of reserve strength. He just could not understand what had happened.

Ben rode on, following the trail of the band. He had not intended to run the horses but wanted to get close enough to see them plainly again, just to make certain he had not missed the black stallion the first time. He wished he had his binoculars but he had not brought them when he came up to Tom Sample's camp. Dixie would bring them when she came, but that did not help Ben now. The horses had halted and were grazing. Ben took advantage of a long hogback and got fairly close to them. There were a black mare, an iron-gray mare, and two dark two-year-old colts, but no black stallion. Ben presently rode directly at them, hoping their fright would bring King from somewhere. They bunched and went away, some of them straggling in a manner which Ben knew King would not have permitted had he been in his customary place.

It was seldom that Ben ever admitted that anything concerning horses was too much for him, but this was. He glanced at the sun, which was already past the midday mark, and headed Inky across the broken country to Little Butte, the appointed place for meeting his father and the riders from Tack. He paid no further attention to the wild band, knowing that, unless it was disturbed, it would make its way to Little Butte water hole of its own accord. His plan had been to wait for it there, then jump it after the horses had watered, and try to separate the black stallion, as he and Dixie and the gaucho had done once before. But now it looked as if that plan would not work.

Ben arrived first at Little Butte. He went into the juniper grove, which was the best place for a camp, unsaddled, and turned his horses loose. They went immediately to the pool, then found sandy places to roll their sweaty backs. Ben inspected the old corral they had used two years before and found it in fair condition. By repairing one place, he believed that he could fix it so it would hold saddle horses, though not a wild stallion. He hunted poles and fixed the fence.

It was nearing sundown when he heard Inky neigh. He hurried out, knowing that, if the wild band was coming, he should catch his horses at once. But it was a little cavalcade coming from the rolling country north of Gailey, and Dixie was in the lead on Gaucho's Listo mare. He waved at her and she waved back. There were three riders, and the spare horses carried packs. Ben soon recognized the other two as the gaucho and Andy Blair.

"Why didn't Pop come?" Ben said. His father did not approve of running wild horses and Ben had wanted him to have a part in this. Also his father was a good bush rider.

"Too busy," Dixie said. "He said four of us ought to be enough."

"Hello, Ben," Mr. Blair said. "I think we should be able to handle it all right."

"Yes," Ben said, "but I wanted Pop to see some of these colts. He won't believe they're as good as they are."

"Maybeso we catch a nice one for take back," the gaucho said, with a wide and happy grin.

"We could do that," Ben said, pleased at the thought. "Come on up to the grove. That's where we'll make our camp."

For the next half hour they were busy, unsaddling, and making camp. Ben was hungry and started a fire, knowing that there was good food in the kitchen boxes.

"Mom send anything?" he asked Dixie.

She nodded, dug into a pack, and brought out a bag of nut-studded chocolate cookies, Ben's favorite food. He took a handful.

"You'd better wait till after supper," she told him.

"This is lunch I'm eating now," Ben said.

Dixie arranged the grill over the coals and got out a bundle of thick steaks. Andy Blair and the gaucho came in from the direction of the water hole.

"We'd better put the hobbles on a little later," Ben said.

"Did you see them today?" Dixie said.

"Yes. But say, Gaucho, King wasn't with them. I can't figure it out."

"No?" the rider said, raising his dark brows. "Where was he?"

"I don't know. I couldn't find him."

"Is he usually with the band?" Andy Blair asked.

"Always," Ben said.

"He wouldn't leave them," Dixie said, positively.

"I rode at them twice, and he didn't show up either time," Ben said.

"It is—how you say it?—funny," Gaucho said.

"It's not very funny," Ben said seriously. "I don't know what to make of it."

"He was with them last night," Andy Blair said. "He must have been, or else Tom would have said something about it."

"Yes," Ben said.

"Oh, you just didn't see him," Dixie said. "He was off on a knoll some place watching you and you didn't see him."

"Could be," Ben said, "but I don't think so. I looked carefully."

"What could have happened?" Andy Blair said. "Is it likely he might have stepped in a hole and fallen."

"Not likely," Ben said. "He was raised up here in these rocks. At least," he amended, remembering that the horse had been born in an Arizona stable, "he's been up here a long time. He knows all about this country."

"Yes, I guess he does," Blair said. "I keep thinking of him as a little colt."

"What time do you think they'll arrive here?" Dixie said to Ben.

"About dark. Maybe after dark, if they smell us and get spooky. I'm pretty sure they'll be in here some time tonight for water. They've been grazing all day and when they get their bellies full of grass they will hit for water."

"Then we will know is the stallion with them," the gaucho said.

"What if it is after dark, in the night?" Andy Blair said.

"We will still know," Gaucho said.

"We'd better get busy and eat," Ben said, taking a dutch oven from one of the saddlebags. "We'll want to hobble our horses before dark."

"Is best for put them in corral so the wild horses no—how you say it?—hesitation," Gaucho said.

"Yes," Ben agreed. "That would probably be better. There will be less excitement."

"But if it's dark, how're you going to tell if the stallion is with them?" Dixie wanted to know.

"If eyes no good, then is time for use ears," Gaucho said, grinning at her.

"Can you hear the color of a horse's hide?" she said.

"Things will be for listening," Gaucho said.

"You'll see," Ben said, though not too certain himself.

Before dark, Ben and the gaucho rounded up the saddle horses and put them in the little corral. A short time later all of them left the grove, crossed the feeble trickle of the creek above the little rock-walled gorge that held the pool, and found places on an upthrust of rock that gave them a good view of the area. The stars were bright and they could make out the dark lines of the walls and the blot that was the grove of trees. Beyond in the darkness lay the rolling brushy country with the distant finger of stone that gave it the name of Standing Rock. Ben strained his eyes in that direction but, after more than an hour had passed, their first knowledge of the approaching herd came in the sound on the rocks.

"There they are," Ben said, in a low voice.

"Where? Where?" Andy Blair asked.

"There's one," Dixie said, her eyes finding a dark form.

"Si," the gaucho said.

"I see them," Ben said. "They're milling around the mouth of the canyon. Now they're coming in to the water."

"Time for hear," Gaucho said in his soft voice.

The horses entered the canyon, moved on to the water hole and out of the line of sight of the four persons on the rocks. But the noise of hoofs on the rocks was borne clearly on the night air. There was the sound of dusty nostrils being sloshed in the water, and then came a splashing as the animals pawed the water to send it up on their legs and bellies. They stayed at the pool for long minutes, obviously taking advantage of this first leisure in drinking that they had known for days. Finally however, in ones and twos, they had their fill and went back to the mouth of the defile. They scattered into the darkness for grazing.

Ben felt a gloomy puzzlement. He could not understand it.

"Is he with them?" Andy Blair asked in a tense whisper.

"No, señor, he is no there," the gaucho said soberly.

"Are you sure?"

"Yes," Ben said. "If he had been there he would have come up to look the place over before the band came in. He would have stood guard on the rim while they were drinking. He would have smelled our horses and neighed a challenge to them. He wasn't with them today and he's not with them now."

"No stallion is with them," Gaucho said.

"Something has happened," Ben said, positive.

Dixie had been thinking, and she said, "Do you suppose Tom Sample could have got him, after we left their camp last night?"

"He wouldn't dare," Andy Blair said.

"He was pretty mad, and so was Pearly Maunderland," Dixie pointed out.

Ben considered the idea, then shook his head. "They couldn't have. I'd have seen them this morning, or some sign of them in Standing Rock. The band was bedded down when I found them; it had been there all night."

"Well," said Andy Blair, perplexed and worried, "what are we going to do?"

The gaucho got to his feet. "Is time for sleep. When morning come we will look. We find him, si."

CHAPTER FIFTEEN

B EN WAS awake the next morning at daylight. He pulled on his pants and boots and made his way to the edge of the grove. He watched while the strong morning light moved swiftly across the brushy land. The wild horses had bedded down beyond the defile which held the pool. Now in the coolness of the morning they got to their feet and began to graze. Ben noticed that two or three suckling colts were back in the band with their mothers. But King was not there. No stallion was with them. However, Ben quickly spotted Tanger, his chestnut gelding.

A step sounded behind Ben and he turned to see the gaucho coming through the trees. The rider halted beside Ben and they watched in silence. Presently Ben spoke. "We might as well catch Tanger," he said.

"Si, señor," Gaucho said. His voice was quiet and his brown face sober, for he knew Ben was disappointed and worried by the absence of the black stallion.

"Now is as good a time as any," Ben said, turning to go back through the trees to the corral for saddle horses.

Gaucho shook his head. "Soon they come for water," he said; "it will be best time then."

Dixie came through the trees. "See anything of King?" she asked.

"No," Ben said.

"Where can he be?" she said, frowning.

Ben shrugged his lack of an answer.

"When chase is close—how you say it?—hot, the stallion sometime he will leave the bunch," the gaucho said.

"Not King," Dixie said stoutly. "He wouldn't leave them."

"Not far, he wouldn't," Ben said. "He would be back long before now. I don't know what could possibly be keeping him."

An injury, such as a broken leg, all three of them knew, could explain the big horse's absence, and in desperate running through the rocks and brush it sometimes happened, but none of them wanted to admit such a possibility. In the silence that followed, the wild horses began, one by one, to make their way toward the defile for the morning watering.

"Now we get the horses," Gaucho said, turning back to the corral.

Andy Blair was making a fire at the camp. "We're going to catch Tanger," Dixie told him as they went by.

When the chestnut went into the little canyon, Ben and Dixie and the gaucho galloped from the trees. Dixie went to the upper end and Ben and the gaucho went to the wider lower entrance. The wild horses inside snorted and came out with a rush and Tanger came with them. Ben drove Inky into the stream and turned Tanger and three others back. They raced along the rocky floor to the upper end, but Dixie was waiting for them there. Back they came and the gaucho let two of the wild ones through.

"Whoa, Tanger, whoa," Ben called.

The chestnut halted and eyed them, while the remaining wild horse, an old mare, crowded close on his heels.

"Slow," Gaucho said. "Is need one little time for remember."

They sat on their horses and Tanger's anxiety decreased rapidly. Ben kept talking to him. The mare stampeded back past the pool and Dixie let her go by.

"Whoa, Tanger, whoa," Ben said, slipping off his horse. Rope in hand, he walked confidently to the chestnut, rubbed the extended nose a few seconds, and then slipped the loop over the horse's neck. "A fine one you are, running off with a wild bunch," he chided gently and turned back to Inky.

A ragged line of dust off to the north showed where the wild horses were when they rode out of the defile. "Turn our horses out to graze a while," Ben told Dixie. "I'll put hobbles on Tanger to make sure he stays around."

Andy Blair had breakfast ready when Ben and Dixie and the gaucho were back at the camp. They filled their plates and squatted around to eat. "It doesn't look so good to me," Andy Blair said presently.

"We'll find him," Ben said. "He's got to be around somewhere."

"That's right," Dixie said. "He can't fly."

The Arizona man considered that briefly, then said, "It still doesn't look good to me," and all of them knew what was in his mind. It was in their minds too. Something had happened to King.

"We'll start right after breakfast," Ben said. "We'll backtrack the bunch into Standing Rock."

"Divide," Gaucho said. "That is best way."

"That's right," Ben agreed. "We'll separate and ride about half a mile apart. In that way we can cover more country."

Andy Blair, looking into the far-reaching distance lying between them and the round dome of old Bell Mountain, said, "It's a mighty lot of country—and a million places for a horse to hide."

"Oh, it's not so big," Ben said, "not when you know it."

"No," Andy Blair said, "I guess not."

"Ben and I have ridden through there a dozen times," Dixie said. "It's King's favorite range."

"He's in there somewhere," Ben said. "He knows every foot of it, all the way from Gailey Ridge to Big Butte breaks."

"Ben will ride ridge, with his far-see glasses," the gaucho said. "I go halfway up, for look in arroyos. Señor Blair ride below."

Ben saw the plan immediately. "That's a good idea," he said. "Then we can cover the whole south slope of Gailey at one time. There are a lot of small canyons in there where he might be. And I can keep watch out in the

flats with my binoculars. One of us ought to spot him."

"Where'll I ride?" Dixie asked the gaucho.

"Dixie will take extra horses and camp to Juniper Springs," the man said. "We stay there this night."

"Oh, no," Dixie said, dismayed. "I want to hunt for King."

"I'll take the extra horses," Andy Blair said. "Dixie will likely be more valuable than I am in the brush anyway."

Ben shook his head. "You don't know where Juniper Springs is," he said. "You might miss it. You'll have to take them, Dixie."

"Oh, all right," she said. "I'll do it—this time."

They finished breakfast, saddled the horses, and put up the packs. "Take your time, Dix," Ben said, when everything was in readiness. "You've got lots of time. Turn the horses loose to graze when you get there, and we'll take off the packs when we get in."

"I'll look after this," she said, tossing her head. "You find King."

"We'll do our best," Ben assured her.

It required an hour for Ben to reach the first high shoulder of the ridge. He halted here and took out his glasses. Far to the north he found dots that he knew to be the wild horses. They were feeding so slowly that they did not seem to move at all. Another band of horses was visible well along Gailey's flank, and Ben made a mental note to have a good look at them later. It was possible that King, separated by the running from his own bunch, had moved in with another band. Further survey of the country to the north showed only a distant band of feeding antelope.

Turning his attention to the other side of Gailey, Ben soon spotted the gaucho below him. The little rider came up out of a canyon, topped the ridge and went down into another canyon, and Ben knew that Gaucho, in assigning the day's riding, had kept the most difficult job for himself. All day long it would be up and down for him, in and out of canyons, searching the twists and turns for the black stallion. When night came that big bay Keister colt would know he had been ridden. Far beyond the gaucho, where the ridges twisting down from Gailey disappeared into the basin, there was another rider and Ben knew it was Andy Blair. Holding to the first upturns, Blair could watch for tracks and look up into the mouth of each successive canyon.

Turning his glasses on out into Standing Rock, Ben could see a little cavalcade of loose and packed horses, heading directly for Juniper Springs, which it would reach long before they did. This was the easiest task of all, but Ben knew that Dixie wasn't happy with it.

Midafternoon found Ben well along the ridge and in a position almost directly above a strange band of wild horses that he had noticed earlier. It was a small bunch. As near as Ben could determine, there were six mares, three suckling colts, four yearlings, and a stallion. The stallion was a sorrel and Ben judged, from the way the band grazed, that it had not been disturbed for several days, which meant that King had not been in the vicinity.

The sun was nearing the crest of Crystal Mountain, far

to the west, when Ben rode into Juniper Springs. The unsaddled horses were feeding on the grassy flat south of the water hole and Dixie and Andy Blair were resting on bedrolls near a small fire. Ben pulled his bridle and saddle off Buck before going to the camp.

"Well, what luck?" Dixie called hopefully.

Ben shook his head. "I saw quite a few horses, but King wasn't with them. You remember the sorrel stud? His band is over north of the ridge. I thought maybe King had moved in on him, but he hadn't. Did you find anything, Mr. Blair?"

"No," the man said, "nothing but three antelope and two coyotes. I didn't see a horse."

"Any tracks?"

"None that looked fresh. It's like looking for a needle in a haystack."

"I saw two mares and colts," Dixie said. "They were out of King's bunch. One of them was the black mare with the saddle marks. You know her, Ben."

"Where were they?"

"About six miles back, west of Standing Rock. I rode over to them. One of the colts is pretty lame."

Ben considered this a few seconds, then said, "I don't think it means much. They probably dropped out before Tom jumped the bunch the last time. We had better get started on supper."

"Maybe the gaucho will know something," Dixie said.

"It'll be late when he gets here," Ben said. "He was pretty well back last time I saw him."

Supper was keeping warm on the rocks and it was after dark when they heard the gaucho ride in. He unsaddled, turned his horse loose, and came into the circle of the light. "Hola!" he said, the irrepressible grin on his dark face. "She is rough country, no?"

"You find anything?" Ben said.

"Si, mio amigo," Gaucho said. "Rocks, sage hens, bobcats—but no black stallion."

"What do you think, Gaucho?" Andy Blair asked seriously.

"He is not there," Gaucho said.

"But where could he be?"

"He's not over in Bascomb Flats," Ben said. "There's another stallion and his bunch there."

"There would be a fight?" Andy Blair guessed.

"Before now, if King had seen them," Ben said. "He'll move right in on the first bunch he sees."

"Unless, of course, he is hurt," the man said.

There was a brief jarred silence, for Ben and Dixie and the gaucho had been avoiding any admission of this possibility, even though, from the facts as they knew them, it was the only logical explanation of the stallion's disappearance. They hoped against it and refused to let themselves believe it. But now that Andy Blair had brought up the subject, the only answer Ben could give was, "Yes." An injured horse does not go around looking for fights.

"We will look in Standing Rock country tomorrow," Gaucho said. "Is good chance for him."

"And I'm going, too," Dixie declared. "There's no use changing camp every day."

"Okay," Ben agreed. "But we'd better fix some sandwiches to take along. It might be a long day before we get back."

They were saddled and ready to ride by sunup the following morning. Ben waited for the gaucho to give each rider directions, but the little man, after obviously thinking the matter over, said, "The canyon trap, is it far, Ben?"

"About three miles, I guess," Ben said.

"We will go there," Gaucho said.

"But there's nothing there," Ben said. "I was over there day before yesterday. There's nothing in the trap. Tom and his men didn't even get the horses in the canyon. The upper fence hasn't been put up."

"We will go there first," the gaucho repeated.

Ben, being the most familiar with the country, led the way through the brush. He took them first to the rim, where they could look down into the shallow canyon. There were no horses in it, not even any tracks except the old ones made by the runners and Ben himself when they had repaired the lower fence. Ben pulled up, but the gaucho, with hardly a glance into the canyon, turned along the rim toward the upper entrance. When he came to the maze of sign where the wild horses had milled before breaking back, he halted. His eyes searched the ground.

"I've been over all this, Gaucho," Ben said, somewhat impatient.

The South American did not reply, but presently pointed to a track made by a shod hoof.

"That's Tanger," Ben said. "He was with them at the time."

"Tom's horses were shod, too," Dixie said.

Gaucho nodded. He studied the tracks for some time and presently dismounted. "Is track of stallion, no?" he said, pointing to a circular depression in the dry earth and looking up at Ben.

"It could be," Ben said. "I couldn't say for sure. It's big enough, but I couldn't be sure."

"He was here," Dixie said. "This is where Tom jumped them, and I am sure King was here."

Leading his horse, the gaucho began to move in widening circles about the area. He kept his gaze on the ground, studying the tracks. The others sat on their horses and watched. Ben felt they should be riding on, but he said nothing. The gaucho had his own way of doing things. After a time he spotted a still form in the brush and said, "What is?"

"That's the old lead mare," Ben told him.

"When she wouldn't go in the trap, they shot her," Dixie said.

Gaucho led his horse over and looked at the dead mare. Ben, Dixie, and Andy Blair stayed where they were. Coming back, the gaucho stopped and picked up something from the ground. His intent study of it aroused Ben's curiosity and Ben rode over to see what it was, followed by Dixie and Andy Blair. The gaucho had the empty brass case of a rifle cartridge.

"That's probably the shell they used to kill her with," Dixie said, bitterness coming into her voice. "I'll bet Pearly Maunderland did it."

The gaucho glanced up at her, a frown on his brown forehead.

Then Ben remembered. He slapped a hand against his thigh and felt the round oblong object in his pocket. "Say," he said, "I found one, too. The other day when I was here . . ." He pulled the case out of his pocket. Gaucho reached for it and examined them both, side by side.

"They shot her twice," Dixie said.

Gaucho shook his head. "Is only one hole."

"Perhaps the first shot missed," Andy Blair said. "What difference does it make? She is dead."

Gaucho turned his dark eyes to Ben and said, "Where you find?"

"Why," Ben said, glancing around to locate the place, "why, it was over there—over there near that big clump of brush."

"We see," the gaucho said.

Ben tried to find the little depression the cartridge had lain in, but apparently he had destroyed it, either in picking up the cartridge or with his feet afterward. This carelessness annoyed him and he said, "It was right here."

"Is sure?" Gaucho said.

"Yes," Ben said. "It was right about here. Here, here're the tracks made by my horse."

Gaucho looked at the tracks, then raised his head and looked over the brush toward the spot where the dead mare lay. Suddenly Ben realized what was in the South American's mind.

"It couldn't have," Ben said, his eyes widening. "She was running from the other direction. A shot fired from here couldn't have killed her. It's too far. No one would have been crazy enough to try a shot like that."

"Perhaps this shot was fired at a coyote or something," Andy Blair said. "That could be."

"Yes, it could be," Ben said, but his answer was slow and thoughtful. "Here, Gaucho, let me see those shells." They were of the same caliber, almost identical in appearance, and neither had lain in the dust very long.

The gaucho got on his horse and began to ride slowly about the spot. Ben knew what the rider was looking for and joined him. They rode in widening circles until they were nearly three hundred yards from the place where Dixie and Andy Blair waited. "I don't see anything," Ben said presently.

"Is nothing," the gaucho said and turned his horse back to the others.

"But why did they do it?" Ben said, turning his horse beside the gaucho's.

"You know maybe—how you call it?—creasing?" Gaucho said.

"Yes," Ben said. Creasing was a term used by horse-runners for trying to stun a horse with a bullet so they could get a rope on it. The purpose was to send the bullet high through the horse's neck but close enough to the spinal cord to bring temporary unconsciousness. Requiring almost perfect shooting under favorable conditions, the practice had proved so difficult and unreliable that it had been almost entirely abandoned years ago. But thinking back, Ben realized that Pearly Maunderland, who always carried a rifle in his saddle boot and liked to brag about his skill, would be just the man to try it. It fitted perfectly with Pearly's character and dovetailed with the things Ben had heard and seen in Tom Sample's camp. It even explained Pearly's cryptic declaration that they, meaning Ben and the Darbys, "would never get" the stallion. A badly hurt horse wanted only to go away and hide.

"What's the matter? What is it?" Dixie asked, genuinely concerned by the black scowl of anger on Ben's face.

"They shot King," Ben said through clenched teeth.

CHAPTER SIXTEEN

T HEY HAD to piece the whole thing together for Andy Blair before he would believe that Tom Sample or somebody in his crew had shot the black stallion. "Everything fits," Ben told Andy. "It was the reason Tom agreed to give up the chase so readily. It was the reason Pearly said we wouldn't get King. Pearly had been after Tom to let him do it; I know that because I heard Pearly say something about 'let me take him,' though I didn't know then what it meant. And the other day, after they failed to get the band into their trap, Pearly was so mad that, with or without Tom's consent, he tried it. Or somebody did."

"I can't believe it," Andy Blair said. "I don't see how anybody could be that brutal and desperate."

"You don't know Pearly Maunderland," Dixie said.

"That was the reason they were all so glum when they got back to Basin Lake," Ben said. "Everything had gone wrong. That's the reason Pearly was so touchy; his shot hadn't worked out. They were almost ready to fight."

"What do you think, Gaucho?" Andy Blair asked.

"Si, señor," the gaucho said soberly.

"But what happened?" Dixie cried. "Did they kill King, too?"

"If they did I'll . . . I'll . . ." Andy Blair's anger was too deep for him to complete the sentence.

"No," Ben said, "I don't think they did."

"He is no here," the gaucho said, nodding at the brush through which he and Ben had ridden.

"The bullet went wild?" Andy Blair suggested hopefully.

"But it hit him," Ben said. "It must have, or he would still be with his bunch. He wouldn't have left them if he weren't hurt."

Gaucho nodded. "He is hurt."

"Oh, oh!" Dixie said, close to tears. "I hate that Pearly Maunderland."

"I'll have him arrested," Andy Blair said.

"What good would that do?" Ben said. "How could you prove anything?"

"There should be some way," Andy Blair said. "He shot one of the best stallions that ever lived."

"But where is King now?" Dixie said.

"Dead, probably," Andy Blair said, his voice bitter.

"Maybe no," Gaucho said. "Is hurt, but maybe no dead."

"Then why isn't he with his band?" Dixie said.

"Is hurt too much," Gaucho said.

Ben nodded. "He probably can't travel."

"Well, where is he? What're we going to do about it?" Dixie said.

[194]

Ben shrugged his shoulders helplessly.

"What can we do?" Andy Blair said, looking around at all the miles of broken brushy country.

The gaucho started his horse.

Ben swung Inky around and said, "Are you going to try to find him, Gaucho."

"Si," the rider said.

"Come on, Dix. Come on, Mr. Blair," Ben said, encouraged by a stirring of new hope. "Spread out. Maybe we can find him."

The gaucho held to the line of sign that led to the southeast, and Ben kept close to him, keeping Inky slightly back in order not to interfere with the rider's study of the ground. Dixie fanned out to the right a couple of hundred yards and Andy Blair rode on the left at about the same distance. The sign was old and confused, the intermingled scuffed tracks left by a bunch of running horses, and Ben did not see how the gaucho could make much of it. But it was their only hope, and the gaucho's resourcefulness had surprised him before.

The gaucho rode slowly, halted occasionally, and was intent in his study of the ground. At places the sign divided and single tracks were clear and distinct through the brush, only to return again to the beaten confusion. Ben saw again and again the shod tracks left by Tanger, but this was of no benefit, for Tanger was back with the extra horses at Juniper Springs. He saw other tracks that he thought might have been left by the black stallion, but he could not be certain.

After they had been riding about an hour, the gaucho raised his head and called to Dixie, "See for one horse track."

"What?" Dixie said, reining up her mare.

"He wants you to watch for a trail left by one horse," Ben yelled at her.

She nodded and they rode on. By now the horses had quit running and had been moving at a walk, showing that they were no longer being pursued and were over their fright.

"They'll begin to graze pretty soon," Ben said.

Gaucho nodded.

"Hey," Dixie shouted. "Here's a single track."

Gaucho looked around, marking his position, then he turned his horse through the brush toward Dixie. Ben followed him. Dixie had found a line of sign, ageless in the dry crumbling crust of the soil. The gaucho looked at it, long and intently. Finally he raised his head and looked through the glimmering heat waves to the southeast. "What is yonder?" he said.

"Where?" Ben rose in his stirrups. "I don't see anything."

"The country?" Gaucho said. "How you say?—what is like?"

"Oh," Ben said. "It's rough—breaks."

"Is water?"

"Yes. Big Butte Creek is over there. It runs through a canyon. I've never been to it but I've seen it from up on Little Butte."

"Okey-dokey," the gaucho said and touched his horse forward.

"Hey, Mr. Blair," Dixie shouted. "Come on." She waved her arm at him.

Ben rode behind the gaucho. "You think this is King's trail?" he said after a few minutes.

"Si," Gaucho said. "I think is."

Ben shrugged but kept silent. Although the gaucho was the smartest horseman Ben had ever known, the gaucho had yet to prove that he was a tracker. Ben's estimation of the brown rider rose a little later however when the gaucho dismounted, wet his finger, and rubbed a small dull spot on a stone. The spot turned bright and then, under continued rubbing, disappeared.

"Blood?" asked Andy Blair, who had come up behind them.

"Si," the gaucho said and remounted.

"This horse is still running," Ben pointed out a short time later.

"Si," the gaucho said.

"But why?" Ben said. "No one was after him here."

"And he was going away from the band," Dixie said.

The gaucho shook his head, indicating that he had no answer.

They rode on through the brush, each silent with his own thoughts. The trail could be followed easily and the gaucho let his horse go at a free-swinging walk. They arrived south of Standing Rock's tall knobby finger in the brassy glare of midday, and the trail led on, straight toward the dry crumbly west rim of Big Butte Canyon.

Some time later the gaucho reined up. The others rode up beside him and they could see a place in the dust where a horse had rolled.

"He stopped here?" Ben said.

"The wound, she hurt," the gaucho said. He dismounted and pointed to places where blood had stained the dry earth.

"He rolled to stop the bleeding," Dixie said.

"Maybeso flies," Gaucho said, getting back into his saddle.

Ben knew it was a common thing for injured animals to try to plaster their wounds with dirt or mud, especially during the season when the flies were bad.

The horse they followed had long since ceased running and as they neared the breaks there was an unevenness in the tracks that told of weakness and wavering. Presently they came to another place where the horse had halted. Here he had not tried to roll but had stood for some time on wide braced legs. And when he moved on, his steps were shorter and the unevenness was greater than before.

"He's hurt bad," Andy Blair said.

None of them answered; there wasn't any answer to the pitiful story told by the scuffed prints in the dry earth.

Now Standing Rock was well behind them and in front they could see the darker ragged line of Big Butte Canyon's far rim, softened in perspective by the heat haze. In all the wild desert-dry land there seemed to be no life, and the hard orange-colored soil threw back the rays of the sun. Dust shifted lazily around the horses' feet.

The halts made by the horse became more frequent. Every hundred yards or so they came to the widened imprints left by braced legs. They came to a place where knee prints were plain in the dust, and to another place where, after falling, the horse had lowered his muzzle to the ground while regaining the strength to get back to his feet.

"He's about finished," Andy Blair said, his voice heavy with sadness.

Centuries of wind and water had hacked the canyon's west rim into a crumbled maze of gullies and arroyos that twisted their way down a half mile's distance between dry jutting ribs of flinty soil. It was an unlovely view of scorched smoky earth relieved only by a strip of green in the canyon's floor.

At the head of one of these ridges the stallion had halted, leaving the prints of his spread feet clear in the dust. And when he had moved on he had done so with a jerky downward trot which in less than twenty feet had ended in a fall. How long the horse had lain there could not be told, but when finally he had struggled back to his feet he had gone on down the ridge, his round hoofs cutting deep into the crumbly soil. Again he fell, and again—and this last time he rolled and slid to the bottom of a slant-walled ravine. They found his hoofprints there, slow short steps, scraping against the narrow walls—walls which held him up and walls against which he lay time after time to rest.

The story of the agonizing struggle was written in the sign.

"My lord!" Andy Blair said. "He never got to water."

They went on, twisting through the narrow passageway, their horses' feet pounding in the same tracks left by the stallion. And they went around each bend with thumping hearts, dreading the minute when they would come upon a black inert form, wedged tight at the base of the walls. But on and on they went, the silent gaucho riding first, Ben next and Dixie third, with sad Andy Blair bringing up the rear, and they rounded bend after bend only to find those staggering hoofprints leading on. And finally, after what had seemed hours, the walls dropped sharply away and the narrow green strip of the canyon floor, with its grass and brush and willows, and its slow-flowing creek, was before them.

The gaucho pushed his horse out into the rich sunlight and halted.

Ben came behind him. "No," Ben said, half to himself, "he never got to water." The dark form lay in deep grass just short of the willows that bordered the creek.

"Oh, King," Dixie said, choking on her emotions.

"I guess it just wasn't meant for me to ever have him," Andy Blair said.

The gaucho urged his horse on. Seeing the black form, the young horse shied away and the gaucho did not press the issue but halted thirty feet away.

"It doesn't look like King," Dixie said.

The black coat was gray with dust, and the mane and tail were matted with dirt. The hip bone stood up prominently and every rib in the gaunt frame could be counted. The bottoms of the feet, extending toward them, were worn until the frog was hardly visible. No, it did not look like King, but it was—and all of them knew it was.

Ben was looking at the bony ribs and suddenly he cried, "He's alive!"

"No, he can't be," Andy Blair said.

"He is. I saw him breathe. Look!"

There was unmistakable movement in the black chest.

"It can't be!" Andy Blair said.

The gaucho swung down and went toward the horse. His feet sank deep in a soft bog under the tall grass.

Then, with a mighty effort, the black horse raised his head, and he looked at them. A fierce, undying fire came into his great dark eyes, but the fire paled and grew dim and the big heavy head dropped back.

"He got to water," the gaucho said. "He is lie in it." He lifted one of his boots, to show them that it was dripping, and added, "Some place is new beaver dam."

CHAPTER SEVENTEEN

THE BLACK stallion lacked the strength for more than a feeble protest when they cleaned the plastered dirt from his neck to see the wound. It had been a poor shot, low and too far back. Luckily it had missed both the spinal cord and the jugular vein, but the bleeding had been heavy and had lasted over a long period of time.

"He knew he was hurt," Ben said. "That's the reason he headed for this place. He wanted a place where he could hide and there was water."

"He has lost a tremendous amount of blood," Andy Blair said. He turned to the gaucho and said, "Do you think there's a chance to save him?"

The gaucho's dark eyes were thoughtful. "Quien sabe? How you say it?—who know? Is bad hurt."

"Sure we can," Dixie said stoutly. "He's alive, isn't he?"

Andy Blair shook his head. "I've seen a lot of sick horses," he said. "It might be best to just . . . to just . . ."

"No sir," Ben said. "He's got a chance. We've got to try."

Andy Blair looked questioningly at the gaucho.

"Si," the little man said, jerking his head in a short nod. "Is good for try."

"But . . . here in this bog?" Andy Blair said. "And we can't possibly move him. He is too weak to walk, and you wouldn't dare drag him."

Gaucho bunched his full lips and glanced around. Then he said, "Ben, go find beaver dam and make hole."

"Sure," Ben said. He hurried away into the willows. It required only a minute to locate the dam. Ben pulled off his boots and socks and got in the water with a long pole. In a few minutes the water was pouring through a sizable hole in a small torrent.

When he got back to the horse, the gaucho was saying, ". . . would be good for horse doctor come."

Dixie stood up. "I'll get one," she said. "I'll go after one."

"No veterinarian will come way out here," Andy Blair said. "It must be a hundred miles."

Dixie closed her lips firmly and said, "He'll come."

"All right," Andy Blair said. "Let me go. That's something I can do."

"Do you think you can find your way back to Juniper Springs?" Ben asked the man.

"Yes, I believe I can."

"Then go get our extra horses and our camp," Ben said. "We'll be here for some time."

Dixie was on her horse. "Come on, Mr. Blair," she said. "I'll ride that far with you."

"And, Dixie," Ben said, "bring a couple of bales of that timothy, and some grain."

"All right." She turned her horse and the two of them rode away, taking the nearest ridge that led back to the mesa.

Ben turned to the gaucho and said, "What'll we do first? Say, the water is going down. It's almost dry here now."

Gaucho nodded, then with a quick hand reached out and jerked Ben to one side, causing him almost to fall. "The heels," he said, nodding to the black horse. "Have big regard for them."

"Aw," Ben said, "he can't kick. He's too sick to kick."

"Always can kick," Gaucho said with sharp emphasis. "Remember all time, is wild horse."

"Yes, that's right," Ben admitted. "I'll be careful. What'll we do first?"

"Fix things for neck," Gaucho said. "Mud, with plenty water."

"I'll get it," Ben said. He went to the creek and searched along its banks until he found a bed of fine yellow earth. He had nothing to mix it in, so got a flat rock. He put clay on the rock and used his hat to carry water to it. Then, with his hands, he worked it into a paste. He carried this back to the gaucho, who tested it with his finger and said, "More water."

Ben brought more water and worked it into the clay. Satisfied with it presently, the gaucho took it to the horse, approaching from the side of the animal's back. He took a handful of the clay and put it gently on the raw wound on the horse's neck, then spread it to a thickness of about an inch. King tried to lift his head and lashed out with a hind foot. Gaucho glanced up to see if Ben had noticed. Ben had, and he knew now that it had been foolish of him to walk close to those heels. King, though hardly alive, was still carrying on his fight against man.

"Hold head," the gaucho said.

Ben went around and knelt on the damp ground near the horse's great bony head.

"Have regard for teeth," Gaucho said.

Ben nodded, remembering the cuts and injuries he had once seen those teeth inflict on a bay stallion. That was when King had won the biggest bunch of mares in Twin Buttes. But the horse before him was a weak and pitiful creature in comparison with the magnificent stallion that had defeated the old bay. Thinking about it, Ben's eyes became misty. King had then been the proudest, strongest, and most beautiful stallion he had ever seen.

Ben reached out blindly and placed his hand on the big flat jawbone. King fought against the touch, but it was easy for Ben to hold the horse's head down. King was as weak as a kitten.

Ben had been wondering how the gaucho would get to the wound on the underside of King's neck. The horse could be rolled over, but he would probably fight and struggle, wasting still more of his strength. But this problem did not worry the gaucho. As soon as he had finished with the top wound he began to dig with his hands in the wet earth under the horse's neck. In a few minutes he had a space large enough for his purpose. King tried to get his head up again when Gaucho cleaned the matted dirt from the wound, but Ben held him still. The gaucho coated the under wound with the soft clay also.

"Is best we can do," the little man said presently, and he got up and went to the creek to wash his hands.

Ben sat there with his hand on the black horse's bony head. He looked at the great sunken caverns above King's eyes and at the looseness of the lips that half hid the long stained teeth, and he felt discouraged and helpless. They had done the best they could, but it wasn't much—and the spark of life in the gaunt thin body was so feeble. King had lost much blood and he had gone for days without food, and now he was so weak that he could hardly raise his head. Ben knew that few range men would have hesitated to do the obvious thing—but he couldn't. He couldn't treat King like an ordinary horse. There was something in King that was too great and too fine.

Somewhere Ben had read or heard that when a human blew his breath into a wild horse's nose the horse was never wild after that. Ben did not believe it, knew in his own mind that it was just one of those old tales that had developed about wild horses, but now, moved by a strong impulse of admiration and affection, he lowered his head and gently blew his breath into King's dusty nostrils. And for some reason the horse chose that minute to open his eyes. It seemed to Ben that the dark orbs had a new expression of peace and confidence.

"King," Ben whispered, "you've just got to get well. You've got to." And he rubbed the big bony head, scratching softly between the ears in a way that he knew pleased all horses.

Twilight came and Ben and the gaucho, sitting on a little rise where they could watch the black stallion, ate their sandwiches. The horse had not moved since they had put on the clay packs, and it was only by careful watching of the slow rise and fall of his chest that Ben knew he was still alive.

"How're we going to feed him?" Ben said. "He'll have to eat."

The gaucho nodded. "Is problem," he said. "We will see. Is good for rest. Now is very tired."

Ben realized that they could do nothing but wait; time would tell. But the waiting was tedious and exasperating.

"Ben like ride up on flat?" the gaucho said presently. "El Señor Blair, maybeso he is losed."

"He could be," Ben said. Then he added, "No, I'll stay here."

The gaucho caught his horse, saddled and rode up one of the long thin ridges. Presently he was lost in the darkness. Ben left the rise and moved down closer to the black horse. King lay as if he were dead and Ben did not go close enough to disturb him.

It was several hours later when Ben heard horses coming down the ridge in the darkness. He got to his feet and went to meet them. Gaucho was in front, and behind him were

[207]

the horses carrying the packs. Andy Blair brought up the rear. Gaucho led the way to a camping place, near the creek and above the spot where the stallion was.

Andy Blair dismounted wearily. Ben began taking the pack from one of the horses. "Have trouble finding the place, Mr. Blair?" he said.

"Never would have found it, if it hadn't been for the gaucho's fire," the man said.

"Fire?"

"Yes. He made a fire up on the rim."

"For make mate," the gaucho said, grinning. He pulled the little gourd with the silver mouthpiece from his pocket and took a pull at the strong tea.

"Gaucho has to have his mate," Ben said. "I think even I could drink some tonight."

The gaucho started gathering twigs and said, "Will make one more pot."

"How's the stallion?" Mr. Blair asked.

"All right, I guess," Ben said.

"Has he been up—on his feet?"

"No."

Andy Blair did not say anything else and Ben knew what he was thinking—that there wasn't much chance for a horse that could not get on his feet.

They unpacked and unsaddled the horses. Ben drove them up the creek in the darkness, so they would not disturb the stallion. When he came back the gaucho and Mr. Blair were sitting on bedrolls around the tiny fire. Gaucho was nursing his mate gourd in both his brown palms and

Mr. Blair had a cup. Gaucho filled a cup from the black pot for Ben. It was so hot Ben could hardly hold the cup and he let it cool a while before taking a sip. It was, as he knew from having tried it once before, strong and bitter. The gaucho never put sugar in it.

"I don't see how anyone can like it," he said, making a face.

Gaucho grinned. "Is drink for—how you say it?—he-man, no?"

"Maybe," Ben said, but he had to admit that the warm liquid felt good down in his stomach and he finished the cup. It was Gaucho's special drink. He ordered the mate leaves by mail, claiming that they were much better than the tea leaves that could be bought in the local stores.

After finishing the tea, they unrolled their beds. Ben went for a look at King before he turned in. The horse was still in the same position. Ben got some water from the creek and sprinkled it on the clay packs, knowing that they should be kept moist.

It was hours later when Ben awoke. The stars were bright overhead and he could see the silent eroded rims of the canyon. He had the feeling that something was wrong and listened intently. But he could hear only the soft natural noises of the night, the murmur of the stream and the whisper of the wind. He decided presently that it was the gaucho's tea that had caused him to awake. But still he couldn't go back to sleep and the premonition of something unpleasant became stronger and stronger. He raised himself on his elbow and looked at the gaucho's bed, and at

[209]

Mr. Blair's. Both men seemed to be asleep. But Ben's strange feeling persisted.

He put back the covers. He did not bother to put on his shirt and pants but slipped his feet into his boots. He got to his feet and made his way silently down the canyon, to the place where the stallion was. Soon he could see the black bulk of the horse, lying just as it had been. Everything seemed all right and Ben was on the verge of turning back to the camp when he heard a fluttering sound. Frightened, he went forward hurriedly. He found that he was in water, that it was halfway to the tops of his boots. And King's head was in water, one nostril completely covered and water almost up to the other one. What he had heard was King's effort to blow the water out of his nose. Instantly Ben knew what had happened, and he blamed himself for not realizing it would happen. The beavers had repaired the dam.

Ben got down on his knees, got his arms under King's big head and raised it above the water level. The horse struggled briefly, then became still.

"Gaucho! Hey, Gaucho!" Ben shouted loudly.

There was a stirring at the camp, and presently the gaucho's alarmed voice called, "Ben! Que es?"

"Here, here," Ben yelled. "Hurry."

The gaucho came running through the grass, with nothing but his underclothes on. He splashed into the water, halted, and said, "Hola! Is the beaver?"

"Yes," Ben said.

The gaucho went splashing on through the darkness toward the creek.

A few minutes later Andy Blair came plowing through the darkness with long strides. He splashed into the water, stopped, and peered down at Ben. "Ben," he said, "for goodness sakes, what's the matter? What are you doing?"

"Holding up King's head," Ben told him.

"Why?"

"To keep him from drowning. Can't you see?"

Andy Blair was silent a few seconds, then he said, "What can I do, Ben?"

"Go help Gaucho tear a hole in the dam," Ben said. "The beavers plugged it up again."

The man went off toward the creek and Ben could hear him and the gaucho splashing about in the darkness. Presently the water began to recede and Ben realized that he was cold. He was on his knees and his boots were full of water and he was wet to his waist. His teeth started chattering and he could not stop them. King's head was a heavy weight on his arms but he did not let it down until only a trickle of water remained on the ground. Footsteps sounded from the direction of the creek and two wet forms came out of the darkness. Ben thought how funny the gaucho looked in his long underwear.

"Is open, Ben," the gaucho said. "The water, she go through. King is okey-dokey?"

"He's alive," Ben said.

"Go get back in bed," Andy Blair said to Ben. "You're freezing."

Ben went to the camp, picked up his bed and lugged it

back. He spread it on the ground between the black horse and the creek.

"What're you doing?" Andy Blair demanded. "You can't sleep there."

"Yes I can," Ben said. "I'm going to."

"But the ground is wet."

"I've got a waterproof tarp. It's been on wet ground before."

"The beavers may plug up that hole again."

"That," Ben said, "is just the reason I'm going to stay here."

"I'll stay," Andy Blair said. "Let me do it. I'll keep watch."

"Suit yourself," Ben said and started to get between his covers.

The gaucho had been considering the situation and now he said, "Is bueno. Come on, Señor Blair. We—how you say it?—hit the hay."

CHAPTER EIGHTEEN

B EN WAS awake at the first light. The position of the black stallion's legs had changed during the night but otherwise he did not seem to have moved. Ben watched and presently was reassured by the steady rise and fall of the horse's chest. King was still alive.

The gaucho was up and had a cheerful fire going. Ben threw back his covers. The sky above the canyon was washed with yellow gold but the shadows still held the night's accumulated chill. Ben could not find his boots and his clothes were at the camp. He went barefooted through the grass to the creek. As he had expected, the beavers had been at work on the dam, but the water was still going through. Ben took the pole and pried loose the limbs and plastered mud. He watched while the current carried them down the stream.

Breakfast was in pans on the fire and the gaucho was pulling gently at his mate gourd. "Buenos dias, mio amigo," he said.

"Good morning," Ben said. He pulled on his clothes,

noticing that his boots had been up-ended on two sticks near the fire to dry. He crouched near the fire, and spread his hands to the heat.

Andy Blair raised on his elbow in his sleeping bag. "How's the horse?" he asked.

"He's still alive," Ben said.

"Has he tried to get up?"

"No, not that I know about."

Andy Blair lay back down and pulled the covers over his face.

"Breakfast will be ready pretty soon," Ben said.

"I'm not hungry," Andy Blair said. "Don't wait for me."

Ben turned his boots around to aid the drying. The gaucho filled two tin plates from the pans and he and Ben ate. When they had finished, Ben said, "We should put on new plasters, shouldn't we?"

Gaucho said, "Is good thing."

Ben took the dishpan and got a supply of clay. He put in water and mixed it thoroughly. King stirred when the gaucho put the paste on the wounds and, as he had the day before, Ben held the horse's head. He was not sure, but it seemed that King had more strength than on the previous day.

"I believe he's better," he told the gaucho.

"Maybeso," the man said, but there was no encouragement in his voice.

Ben could see that the wet clay had drawn some of the inflammation out of the bullet wounds. The gaucho spread the new paste gently. King's eyelids fluttered and his front feet moved as if he were trying to run.

"Easy, boy. Easy, King," Ben said, in the low voice he used to soothe frightened horses. "We're not going to hurt you. Just take it easy." He rubbed the horse's head and scratched around the base of his ears.

The gaucho finished and settled back on the flat heels of his boots, his clay-smeared hands hanging idly in front of his knees.

"What can we do now?" Ben asked, a bit anxiously.

Gaucho shook his head.

"Maybe he wants water?" Ben said. King needed so much that he felt there must be something they could do.

The gaucho shook his head again. "He have plenty water —last night."

"Yes, that's right," Ben said. "That's one good thing. He had all the water he could take."

"Beaver do—how-you-say-it?—good turn," Gaucho said, a hint of his familiar grin coming to his eyes.

Andy Blair came from the direction of the camp, halting a few feet away to look at the horse with a critical eye.

"He's better, Mr. Blair," Ben said. "I believe he almost tried to get up a little while ago."

"I hope he is," the man said, but there was not much hope in his eyes. "He'll have to get up. He will have to eat."

"I'll feed him," Ben said.

"How?"

"I'll get him some grass. This grass here is too rank and

tough, but there's some good grass back up in the breaks. I'll get some for him."

"I doubt if he'll eat it," Andy Blair said.

"Sure he will," Ben said. "He's hungry. I'll get him some."

He caught Inky, put on his saddle, then emptied the potatoes in a box to get a feed sack. He rode up one of the ridges until he was near the rim. The clumps of grass were scattered and wilted by the summer's heat, but Ben knew there was strength in this sun-cured forage. He began to gather it, cutting the clumps close to the ground with his knife. Inky approved Ben's choice by grazing.

It took Ben more than an hour to fill the small sack. He rode back down the ridge with the sack across his saddle. Gaucho and Andy Blair were at the fire, preparing the noonday meal. Fearing that Inky's nearness might excite King, Ben halted fifty feet away and carried the sack to the place where the stallion lay. He took out a handful of the grass and put it in front of King's nose. King's eyes were dull and tired and he made no effort to eat. Ben pulled the loose lips apart and put a few sprigs of the grass in the horse's mouth. Still King made no effort to chew or swallow. Ben squatted there, discouraged. He realized that he had never learned how to make a horse eat. And King had to eat—just had to, or he would die.

"Food's ready, Ben," Andy Blair called from the camp.

Ben dumped the rest of the grass in front of King's nose, then took Inky's rein and went to the camp. Neither the gaucho nor Andy Blair asked him if King had eaten the grass, and Ben realized that they knew he had not. That was the reason they had not offered to help him gather the grass; they had known it was useless.

After eating, Ben stayed around the camp a long time, doing such odd chores as washing tin plates and gathering dry wood, to pass the time, and hoping and hoping, but when finally he went back to where King lay the pile of grass was just as he had left it. Ben squatted on his heels, discouraged. After a time, the gaucho came and squatted beside him.

"Is difficult thing," the gaucho said.

"Maybe it's too dry," Ben said. "Maybe it's too dusty for him."

He went to the camp and got the big dishpan. He put the grass in the pan and took it to the stream, and he held the pan down so the water would run over the edge. He stirred the grass in the water, then tipped the pan and let the water drain away. He did this again and carried the wet grass back to the horse. He put some in front of King's nose, even put some in the horse's mouth. But King made no effort to eat.

The gaucho got up and walked away.

Tears came to Ben's eyes and he said, "You've got to eat, King. You've just got to." King's eyes opened, but he did not try to eat.

Ben remembered how Inky had chewed the grass, had crushed the fibers with his strong back teeth and had mixed it with the juices of his mouth, and he thought that was what was needed. If there were just some way he could get

Inky to chew grass for King. He even thought of putting a tight rope about Inky's neck to keep him from swallowing, but on more sober thought he knew that would not work. It seemed that nothing would work, but Ben would not give up.

The problem was to find something that King would eat, that he would swallow and which, down in his stomach, would give him strength. But what? King would not eat grass. Ben thought and thought, and then he remembered the big bowls of greens—turnip greens and chard and spinach—that his mother cooked and put on the table at home. He did not like them much but he ate them because his father said they were good for him. And his mother said they had a high food value. That was just what King needed, something with a high food value. Ben wished he had some, a whole tubful, flavored with bacon fat and butter. Maybe King would eat that; it certainly slipped down easily.

This train of thought gave Ben an idea. He got an iron kettle and filled it with the grass and some water. He took it back to the camp and put it on the fire. He put a heavy lid on the kettle, to keep any of the strength from escaping

The gaucho was up the creek, looking after the horses, which of course were all right. Andy Blair was sitting on a bedroll. He watched Ben's preparation to cook the grass, but said nothing. Ben put fresh limbs under the kettle and got the fire hot. He did not know how long his mother cooked spinach but he judged that half an hour would be about right. He had no watch and he did not want to ask

Andy Blair, so he guessed at the time. When he thought it was about right, he pulled the kettle from the fire and let it cool until he could lift the lid. He was amazed at the way the grass had shrunk, and realized that the small amount of wet green stuff in the bottom of the kettle would not make much of a meal for a horse. But he knew it would be good for King, if he could just get it down.

When the greens had cooled, Ben poured them into one of the tin pans and took it to King. He put the pan down in front of King's nose and saw the horse's nostrils swell to take in the smell. Still King did not try to eat. Ben put a gob of the dripping stuff in King's mouth and King's jaws moved and his tongue lifted and then he swallowed.

Ben was elated. He stood up to call Andy Blair to come and see, but just then a hail, "Woooohoooo!" came down the slope. Ben looked up to see Dixie, pushing Listo at a fast walk. There was a man behind her, and behind them was a third horse, carrying a high pack. Ben went to meet them, and the gaucho and Andy Blair angled across from the camp.

"This is Sam Graley," Dixie told them, swinging down from her saddle. "He's a vet."

"What a ride!" the veterinarian, a slight young man, said. He was covered with a fine layer of dust and his face was red from the heat of the upland sun. He looked as if he were about to fall out of his saddle.

"Where's King?" Dixie said.

"Same place," Ben answered.

"Come on, Doctor," Dixie said, leading the way.

Dr. Graley dismounted and stood looking at the black stallion, and a pucker came in his sunburned forehead.

"I want to thank you for coming, Doctor," Andy Blair said. "I know it was a long, hard trip."

"How long has he been like this?" the doctor said.

"Ever since we found him, yesterday," Ben said. "But he took some food. He swallowed some, just a minute ago."

"What?"

"This." Ben went around the horse and picked up the pan containing the cooked grass.

"Ummmm," the doctor said, sniffing at it. He knelt and looked at King's eye. He moved around behind the horse and took the clay pack from the upper neck wound. "Ummmm," he said, looking at the exposed hole. "Pretty good. Not much infection. Bring me some hot water. Dixie, get my bag."

Ben hurried to the fire, poured water in the big kettle, and put it back on the coals. As soon as it was warm, he took it back to the group around the horse. The doctor had cleaned the clay from the horse's neck and now he washed the wound with the warm water and a soft cotton swab, washed until it looked fresh and raw. From his bag he took a big jar of white ointment, and he put this over the wound, on both sides, smearing it on thick. King moved his head and Ben knelt to hold the horse still. King lashed out with his hind foot.

"Well, he's still alive," the doctor said. He took out of his bag a sharp knife and a rubber tube with a metal end. After a few minutes of exploring with his fingers, he made a quick, small cut in King's neck, near the shoulder. He inserted the silver end of the tube into the cut, took a gallon jug full of a thick liquid that had been in the pack, and held it up. "Here, hold this," he said to Andy Blair. In a few seconds the liquid was running from the jug down through the tube and into King's body.

"What's that?" Ben asked.

"Glucose," the veterinarian said. "We've got to get some food into him. This is intravenous feeding."

"Will it . . . will it . . . ?" Ben said, his eyes pleading for a favorable answer.

"It won't hurt him," Dr. Graley said. "That I'm sure of."

A few minutes later the doctor said, "That's enough for now." He put up his instruments and they went to the camp. Dr. Graley threw himself on the first bedroll he saw and said, "Boy, what a ride!"

"We had to get here," Dixie said.

"That's right," the doctor said. "But I hope we don't have to hurry so much going back." He raised up, looked at her, and said, "Aren't you tired?"

"Yep," she said simply.

"Well, then, why don't you look like it?" he shouted. He turned to the others. "She got me out of bed at midnight and we haven't stopped a minute since then."

Ben and the gaucho and Andy Blair scurried about, getting supper. It was almost dark by the time it was ready. Dixie was asleep on a bedroll and they had to wake her to eat. While they were eating, Dixie suddenly put a hand to her shirt pocket and said, "Oh, Mr. Blair—" She handed him a yellow telegram. Andy Blair held the paper to the firelight so he could read it, and when he had finished he said, "I've got to go back to Arizona. Nothing serious, just business. But it's pretty important. Still, I can't go now . . . not until we know about Midnight Chief."

"We can take care of him," Ben said.

"I know you will, but I should be here. After all, he's my horse."

"Yes," Ben said, realizing that in his deep concern he had forgotten that important fact.

A few minutes later Andy Blair reread the telegram and he said, "I really should go. I am sorry, but I should."

"We'll look after King," Dixie said. "You don't need to worry about him."

"When are you going back, Dr. Graley?" Andy Blair said.

"In the morning, if I can get on a horse," the doctor said, groaning as if the very thought pained him. "I've done all I can. I'll leave the tubes and glucose here. From now on, it's just a matter of time and care—and luck."

Andy Blair was thoughtful a few seconds, then said, "I believe I had better go. I don't like to leave at this time, but there are some business matters which should have my attention."

"That's all right," Ben said. "We can let you know when he's ready to—when he's all right again."

"That will be fine, Ben," Andy Blair said. "If you would do that for me, I'd appreciate it."

Ben nodded. "You can take them back to the ranch to-morrow, Dixie," he said.

"Why me?" Dixie said. "Why do I have to do all the riding? You take them."

"Me?" Ben said, shocked. "I've got to look after King. I can't leave."

"I'll look after King," Dixie said. "Gaucho and I can take care of him. Can't we, Gaucho?"

"We can go back alone," Dr. Graley said. "I think I can find the way back."

"No," Ben said. "One of us will go with you. We might as well take back a lot of these extra horses while we're at it. The feed's none too plentiful here anyway."

"I will do it," the gaucho said. "Is good job for me."

CHAPTER NINETEEN

WITH THE little horseman from South America in the lead, the string of horses, some carrying riders and pack equipment and others bare, moved up the narrow knife-edge ridge. Each was silhouetted in turn against the high blue of the sky, and then disappeared beyond the canyon's crumbling rim, leaving a slow drift of thin dry dust to slide across the sun's strong light. Above the camp, Inky, safe in hobbles, questioned the parting with an anxious neigh.

"Hush up, Inkpot," Dixie said, with hearty good cheer. "What are you complaining about? You haven't anything to do but keep your belly full. Well, Benjamin, what's the first thing on the program?"

Ben was aware of a feeling inside somewhat akin to that expressed by Inky. He felt an annoying lonesomeness and knew that the job he and Dixie had assumed for themselves looked much bigger, now that the capable gaucho and the veterinarian were gone. But this was no time to think about that. "Come on," he said to Dixie. "I'll show you the dam." He led the way past King and through the willows to the creek bank.

"You may have to open it," he told her, "if the beavers plug it up again."

Slim and straight in her worn riding clothes, Dixie, except for her yellow hair and unmistakably feminine face, looked like another boy. She listened intently.

"Here's the pole you do it with," Ben said. "You put it in under the limbs and pry, like this. You might have to get in the water."

"I can do it," she said, nodding her head determinedly.

"In a way it's a good thing," Ben explained, "because it means that King can get plenty of water. All he has to do is let it run in his mouth and that's something he needs. But if it backs up too deep, it might drown him. We have to watch out for that."

"What else?" Dixie said.

"And we have to keep feeding him through that tube, like the doctor said," Ben said. "And keep fresh ointment on his neck."

Dixie nodded. "What else?"

"Well, well, I guess that's about all," Ben said.

"Nothing to it," Dixie said.

"Well, it's mighty important," Ben said, nettled by her manner.

"Sure," she said. "Now you go get the camp cleaned up."

Ben frowned at her. "What're you going to do?"

"I'm going to stay here with King a while," she said. "I haven't seen him much lately."

That first day was a long, trying one. As he washed the breakfast dishes and tidied up the camp, Ben's feeling of loneliness and helplessness increased. So much was at stake, King's very life, and there was so little he could do. When Dixie returned to the camp in midmorning her face was sober, and Ben knew that for the first time in her life her strong spirit was flagging.

"He's a mighty sick horse, Ben," she said.

Ben nodded. "Has he been moving about any?"

"No."

Dr. Graley had given the horse a glucose feeding that morning before he left, and two additional times during the day Ben and Dixie fitted the rubber tubing over the little silver nozzle which the veterinarian had left held by adhesive tape in the horse's neck. They watched anxiously while the level of the liquid decreased in the jug. The rise and fall of King's chest was regular, but he showed no interest in living.

"He's so thin," Dixie said, as she rubbed the big black head.

"Watch out for his teeth," Ben cautioned.

"He won't bite me," she said.

"Just the same, keep your hand away from his mouth," Ben ordered. "And don't ever get in reach of his heels. He may be sick, but he's still a wild horse."

The beavers started work on their dam at dusk and Ben let the water back up until it was lapping around King's loose lips and a couple of inches deep against his side, then he went to the dam and pried open the newly closed hole.

He watched while the level of the water receded, but there was a discouraging indifference about the big black horse.

Both Ben and Dixie brought their beds down near King that night and just befor daylight Ben had to open the dam again. While he worked, he could hear the snub-nosed beavers slapping their tails in the pond.

Three times again that day they fed King glucose through the tube, and when night came the last jug was half empty.

"That was all Dr. Graley had in his office," Dixie said. "One of us will have to go in and get some more."

"It doesn't seem to be doing him much good," Ben said.

"It is," the girl insisted. "He's still alive, isn't he?"

"Yes, but . . ."

"And he's stronger, too."

"How do you know?"

"I just know," she said. "He is. We've got to keep feeding him. I'll go after more. I'll start early in the morning."

They got up early the next morning, before daylight. Dixie went to the camp, made a fire, and cooked breakfast while Ben opened the beaver dam. They did not talk, because there seemed to be nothing to say. After breakfast, Dixie took her bridle and went up the canyon to catch Tanger. Ben knew it would be a long day so there was no use in hurrying to clear up after the meal. He went down to the grass patch. King did not seem to have changed position during the night. Ben squatted on his heels, looking at the horse, and his young face was sober. For a time he did not actually see the horse, so engrossed was he with his thoughts, then gradually the feeling came to him that something had changed. There was something about the place, familiar in all of its details because of his long hours of watching, that was different. What was it? Ben stood up, his attention now thoroughly aroused. What had happened? Suddenly Ben let out a yell. "Dixie!"

Dixie was at the camp, and at Ben's cry she dropped Tanger's reins and came striding through the wet grass. "What is it? What's the matter?"

"He ate," Ben cried. "He ate. He took some food."

"He did?" She came to a halt, at first delighted, then her brow puckered into a frown. "How do you know?"

"Do you remember that grass? I cooked part of it for him. Don't you remember? I was trying to feed it to him when you got here with the vet. Don't you remember?"

Dixie thought briefly, then shook her head. "No. I guess I didn't see it."

"Aw, you must have," Ben insisted. "It was here—right here!" He pointed to a place near King's head.

"Well, what about it?" she said.

"It's gone! Can't you see? It's gone!"

"Oh, you think he ate it?"

"Sure he did. What else could have happened to it?"

"Maybe the beavers got it?" she said slowly.

"Beavers don't eat grass. At least, I don't think they do. I never saw them eat anything but tree bark."

"Maybe something else came along, chipmunks or ground squirrels."

"No. It would have to be a dozen squirrels, to eat it all.

We've got to get him some more. We'll open one of those bales of timothy you brought."

"Maybe Tanger came down during the night, or Inky," she said.

Tanger or Inky would have eaten the grass, Ben could not deny that. "But . . . where are the tracks? We should see the tracks."

"Maybe the water washed them out, when it backed up," she said.

"No it didn't," Ben said. "King ate it. He must have."

Dixie glanced up at the sky, which was now streaked with gold above the canyon and said, "I'd better get started, if I'm going to get back by tomorrow night."

"Bring some more hay," Ben said.

"You keep giving him that glucose, till it's all gone," she said.

Dixie saddled, rode up the narrow ridge and disappeared over the rim. But Ben did not feel alone; his mind was busy. There had been a lot of the grass, more than a hatful, he believed. Of course that wasn't much for a horse to eat; Inky or Tanger would have made short work of it. But it was a lot for King, a lot for a horse that had not eaten for nearly four days, perhaps longer than that. It had been right there; King would not have had to move his head very far to get it. He could have reached it without any trouble. It had been right there, even a few wet sprigs of it were still there. Ben wished he had seen them before, so that he could have shown them to Dixie.

"You ate it, didn't you, King?" he said. But the horse,

though his eyes were open, appeared to be almost asleep.

Ben went to the camp and took the tarpaulin from the two bales of hay and the small sack of grain that Dixie had brought. He broke one of the bales and took an armful of the succulent timothy to King. His father cut a small patch of it each year for bailing, and it was the best horse feed Ben knew. King's nostrils widened as he drew in the smell of it, but he made no effort to eat. Ben watched for an hour, but still King didn't eat.

When Ben went back to the camp, Inky was picking around the edges of the tarpaulin. Ben gave him a small block of the hay. "But you stay away from King," Ben warned. "Don't you bother his hay." And just to make certain that he did not, Ben took the horse above the camp and put light hobbles on him. He would tie him to a tree that night.

Ben stayed away from King till after the noon meal, hoping desperately that when he went back the hay, or at least a portion of it, would be gone. It wasn't, except perhaps a few twigs. Ben shook his head sadly. He attached the rubber tube and gave King about a third of the glucose that remained. Later in the afternoon he gave him half of the rest of it, saving the other half for the next morning, because he knew that Dixie would not return until late in the day.

Ben had his supper, took a look at the beaver dam, and got into his bed. He lay for a while, looking at the stars and listening to King's breathing. There was comfort in the fact that the horse was still alive, but Ben realized the present condition could not last much longer. King either had to get better, or . . . or . . .

Ben was awakened by water running into his bed. "Doggone those beavers," he said, sitting up. "I wish they would work in the daytime." He pulled his bed out of the water, so it would not become soaked, then went to the dam and pried the hole open.

It was much too late to get back into a wet bed, so Ben went to the camp and made a fire. He made himself comfortable against his saddle and dozed. It was broad daylight when he awoke. He got up, made another fire, and had his breakfast. He went to look at King, and stopped a dozen feet away. Then he looked quickly at Inky, tied to a tree up the canyon, and cried to King, "You ate it! You did!" The pile of hay was gone.

Ben's heart was singing as he went back to camp. He threw the tarpaulin from the hay and gathered a big armful. He took this back to King, dumping it not far from the horse's head. King's eye was brighter than it had been for days. Ben could hardly contain himself. The big horse was going to get well. Ben wanted to shout and yell, but there was no one to hear him, no one except Inky. He went up and turned Inky loose. "Your pop's going to make it, Inky," he said. "He's going to be all right." The gelding put his head down and began to graze.

Ben went back to King, unable now to stay away. The horse still lay in the same position, but Ben knew he was better. Ben fixed the rubber tube and gave the horse the last of the glucose. Then he took the silver tube from the horse's neck, put a square of clean gauze over the hole and taped it down firmly with adhesive, as the veterinarian had told him to do. He cleaned the neck wounds, noticing that they had almost closed, and put on fresh ointment.

Dixie came pushing Tanger through the slanting sunlight, with a high-laden pack horse behind her. Ben rode to meet her.

"What's the matter? What're you doing up here?" There was anxiety in her voice. She had been riding steadily and a thin coating of dust had settled on her clothes.

"I thought I'd better meet you," Ben said. "I didn't want you to go blundering down into the canyon."

"Why not?"

"Come on," Ben said, "and I'll show you." He turned and led the way to the rim and down the trail. A dozen yards back from the shoulder that permitted them to see the bottom, he halted and dismounted. "Get down," he said.

"Is he . . . ?"

"You'll see," Ben said, and went forward on foot.

Dixie was at his side and presently they could see down to the bottom of the canyon.

"Ben! Ben, he's up!" Dixie cried.

A gaunt black horse was standing on wide legs near the center of a beaten area of rank marsh grass, standing with his head down, eating from a pile that was nearly two bales of good timothy hay.

CHAPTER TWENTY

A NDY BLAIR halted his big heavy car, horse trailer attached, in the yard. There was a happy smile on his
face. Vince Darby went to greet him and they shook hands.
"I got your letter, Vince," Andy Blair said. "I could hardly
believe it. I thought Midnight Chief was dead weeks ago."

"No, he's all right," Vince said. "From what Ben tells
me, he's coming back in good shape."

Andy Blair shook hands with Ben, and then with Dixie.
"I don't see how you did it," he said to them. "I thought it
was hopeless."

"Shucks," Ben said, somewhat embarrassed, "it would
take more than that to kill King."

"He grew up with the wild horses," Dixie said. "Wild
horses don't die easily."

Andy Blair nodded. "Maybe that makes a difference. I'll
see to it that you are well paid for your time and effort."

Ben shook his head. "We didn't do it for pay."

"No, we couldn't take any money for that," Dixie said. "We just couldn't take any money for saving King."

"I'll take care of that," Andy Blair said. "Where is he? I want to see him."

"He's still up in Twin Buttes," Vince Darby said.

"We didn't bring him down," Ben said. "We wanted to let him get as strong as possible."

"You've got him in a pen?" Andy Blair guessed.

Ben shook his head and said. "He's running loose. He wouldn't do well in a pen."

"What do you mean—wouldn't do well?"

"He would fret and worry," Ben said. "It would take him longer to get strong."

Andy Blair was silent, then said, "Oh, I see. But how are we going to catch him? Did you tame him?"

"No sir," Ben said. "We never put a rope on him. He would fight it as sure as anything; and, weak as he was, we didn't want to take a chance of hurting him—not until we just had to."

"But are you sure you can find him?" Andy Blair said, beginning to be concerned.

"Sure," Ben said. "He's in Big Butte Canyon. We won't have any trouble in finding him."

"Three of our horses are there with him," Dixie said. "We left them to keep him company. They're good friends now. King thinks they're his own bunch. We left an old mare hobbled. They won't leave her."

"But how'll we get him down here?" Andy Blair asked, directing the question to Vince Darby.

"Ben and Dixie have it figured out," Vince said. "I reckon maybe they can do it. They know him better than anyone else does."

"When we bring the other horses down, I believe he'll follow, if we just give him a chance," Ben said. "He's been with them a long time now. I believe he'll come right to the corrals and maybe, if we tie the others up inside and leave the gate open, he'll come right in."

"I bet he will," Dixie said confidently, "especially if there is a rack full of hay. You would never believe the way he has gotten to be a hay hound, Mr. Blair."

"I can," Vince said. "You've packed up there practically all the timothy I had in the barn."

Andy Blair laughed delightedly. "Timothy is none too good for that horse, Vince. Name your own price for it. When can we go up and get him, Ben?"

"Any time you wish," Ben said.

"Tomorrow? How about in the morning?"

"All right," Ben said.

"You'll go with us, Vince?" Andy Blair said.

Vince shook his head. "I don't think it will be necessary. But I'll be here to help you load him."

"I'm going," Dixie declared.

"I figured you would," her father said. "They couldn't do anything with King without you along."

"I know how to handle him," she said, unabashed.

"You sure do," Andy Blair agreed. "Where's the gaucho? I doubt if we ever would have found Chief if it had not been for him."

"He's out working a colt," Ben said.

"I've got a supply of mate for him, straight from the Argentine," Andy Blair said. "And, say, there are a couple of nice saddles in the back of my car. One of them should be about a fit for you, Ben, and the other one is just right for a certain young lady I know. Think you could use it, Dixie? You'd better get them out and get the stirrups adjusted to the right lengths."

But even the good new saddle he was riding could not keep Ben from feeling a certain sadness late the next afternoon as he and Dixie and Mr. Blair, with a spare horse to carry their bedrolls, approached the crumbling rim of Big Butte Canyon. During all the weeks they had been caring for the black stallion and watching him grow back to strength and beauty, Ben had been pushing this very day out of his mind, had put it off as something of the future, and hopeless to worry about. But it wasn't of the future any longer; it was here—the present. From the lack of conversation on Dixie's part for the past few hours, he knew that she was worrying too. It was almost unbelievable for Dixie to be silent so long, and Ben was glad that Andy Blair, happy and jubilant over the prospect of seeing his horse, did not notice her preoccupation. Ben tried to brighten up, to be cheerful and talkative, but he made such a poor effort that Dixie looked at him with a sour expression.

"After all these years, I'm going to have Midnight Fire's blood back in my colts," Andy Blair said. "You just can't realize what this means to me, Ben. It's more than money.

There is something about raising fine horses that just doesn't have any connection with money. Of course, I have to sell them, or I couldn't stay in business. But it's the producing of something fine and beautiful that is important. When you're older you will probably understand what I mean, if you stay in the livestock business."

"Yes sir," Ben said. "I expect to be a rancher."

"You'll probably concentrate on cattle," Andy Blair said. "I doubt if there is the same thrill in raising them that there is in horses."

"No sir," Ben said.

"There's just something about horses," Andy Blair said. "I don't know just how to explain it. But horses get into your blood."

"Yes sir, they sure do," Ben said. He did not know just how to explain it either, and right then he did not have the heart to try. He knew he was not thinking about the same horses Andy Blair was. He was not thinking about sleek, trim racing horses, with their box stalls and fancy blankets and grooms; he was thinking about desert mustangs, wind-whipped mesas and lonely water holes. He was thinking about horses that had to fight for every chance, even for life itself. He was thinking about a great black stallion who, so superbly fitted to be a leader, had earned a kingdom in the wild, free, high country and now was to have that kingdom taken from him. He did not have the heart to try to explain this because he knew it was something that Andy Blair, a stud-farm man, could not understand. Andy Blair did not know the sweep and glory of the high country.

"We'd better take it easy," Ben said. "We don't want to get him excited."

"He's only used to Ben and me now," Dixie said.

They threaded their way down the narrow trail and Ben pulled to a halt on a ridge shoulder that gave them a view of the canyon floor. Almost instantly a neigh, strong and challenging, came ringing up the broken wall.

"There he is," Dixie said, unable to keep the thrill of pleasure out of her voice.

Four horses were in the green bottom of the canyon, all with their heads up and their ears pointed up the slope, but one drew their eyes like a magnet. Standing tall on muscular legs, black against the green, he was a shining picture of natural grace and untamed spirit.

"He's beautiful," Andy Blair said. "There's something about him that I have never seen in another horse—not even in Midnight Fire."

"He's wild," Dixie said. "I don't care where he was foaled, he's a wild horse."

Ben touched his horse on down the trail. The black stallion came to challenge them, lifting his front feet high in truculent strides. He halted at the foot of the slope and sent another strong neigh up at them.

"He's feeling that timothy hay," Dixie said.

"Yes," Ben said. "It's a good thing you didn't wait any longer, Mr. Blair. A couple of more weeks and this canyon would be too small to hold him. He'd have to have a lot more country."

Andy Blair did not answer. He seemed unable to take his eyes from the stallion. King neighed again, his big, dark nostrils flaring wide.

"Oh, shut up," Dixie said. "You know we're not going to hurt you."

As they rode on down the trail, the stallion retreated up the canyon toward the other horses, which had now returned to their grazing. He rounded them up and drove them on before him.

"He always does that," Dixie explained to Andy Blair. "But they won't go far. Those gentle horses won't go far. And anyway, not the one with hobbles on."

They crossed the canyon floor to the now-familiar camp spot.

"I see the beavers have their dam in good shape," Dixie said, looking at the water backed up in the marsh grass. New grass had sprung up to hide the place where King had lain.

Near the gray ashes of the previous fires they unsaddled their horses and turned them loose. The horses drank, rolled their sweat-darkened backs, and then went trotting up the canyon to find the others.

"Aren't you afraid they might leave?" Andy Blair said.

Ben shook his head. "They know there's a bale of hay here," he said, and set about gathering dead limbs for the fire.

Before dusk the horses were back. The ranch horses

came in close to the camp, but King, giving occasional anxious little snorts, remained farther back. Ben broke the bale of hay. Some he scattered among the waiting mares and geldings and the rest, a big armful, he took on farther into the flat. The stallion retreated, a nervous dark shape. Ben threw the hay down and came back to the fire. One of the geldings left the little bunch and started for the pile but before he reached it King appeared and the gelding came back.

It was a quiet camp. No one, not even Andy Blair, had much to say, and soon after they had eaten they unrolled their beds and turned in. Ben was up at daybreak the next morning. They fixed breakfast and while Dixie and Andy Blair cleared away, Ben caught their saddle horses. They saddled and packed, and then Ben caught the other three horses, leaving only King loose. The stallion retreated up the canyon and whinnied anxiously. All this was not as it had been before and he was nervous and perturbed.

"You think he'll follow?" Andy Blair said, his eyes uncertain.

"I think he will," Ben said. He mounted and led the string of horses across the canyon floor and up the ridge trail.

King became deeply alarmed. He whinnied and neighed and ran from the creek to the wall in a thundering gallop and back again.

Andy Blair turned in his saddle and Ben said, "Keep on coming. Don't pay any attention to him."

They rode up the trail and reached the rim. King's excitement and consternation echoed repeatedly from the walls behind them. They were nearly half a mile from the rim when the stallion's neigh sounded clear and distinct.

"He's coming, Ben, he's coming!" Andy Blair said, his voice lowered in his own excitement.

"Yes," Ben said, but he did not turn to look back.

King neighed again and again, calling to the horses in front. He could not understand why they went away from him, why they accompanied men. All of his life he had feared men, had fought them and distrusted them. But these horses he had run with and had come to know and regard as his own band now went with them, willingly and without complaint. King was perplexed and disturbed. But still his attachment for the horses and his dislike of being left alone caused him to follow. His nervousness was expressed in his neighs, but the animals in front moved on in stolid indifference and no one seemed to have the slightest interest in him. Gradually his neighs became less frequent and less hopeful, and after a time they ceased entirely. Still he followed, driven by gregarious instinct and encouraged by the indifference with which the men seemed to regard him. He had not yet fully regained his strength and the steady traveling began to tire him. His head dropped lower and lower, losing its proud challenging carriage, and by midmorning, a quarter of a mile to the rear, he was merely matching the steady progress of the horses in front.

Ben looked back, but only once. He couldn't stand it. That wasn't King back there, that wasn't a wild stallion, proud and protective of his band. That was just a horse, a confused, lonesome horse, deprived of what had made the blood race through his veins and put the wild lordly challenge in his neigh—that was just a horse, just Midnight Chief. And he, Ben Darby, had helped to do it. Ben looked back only once.

Dixie did not look back either, and there was only silence, depressing and unrelieved, among the three of them as they rode through the brassy sunlight of the high desert. Ben wound in and out of the brush, dropped into ravines and coulees and climbed out opposite sides, but held a steady course for Gailey Ridge's broken nose. They planned to reach Tack by four o'clock. It would take a while to get the black stallion in the corral and a while to get the necessary ropes and hobbles on him, but with his father and Steve and the gaucho helping it should not take too long, and Andy Blair could leave that night if he wanted to. And when the trailer, hooked behind the big car, bounced up the rough, narrow road and over Crystal Canyon's rim it would be over—all over. Then Ben could start thinking about something else, like getting ready to go back to Boise for school. It would be only a couple of weeks before the summer would be gone.

Dixie pushed her horse up beside Ben and said, "There's a wild bunch—over yonder."

"Where?" Ben said, instantly alert. That was the one danger in taking King down loose.

"Over there, against Gailey," Dixie said.

Ben looked. A dozen or so dark forms were against the

flank of one of the spurs that came down from Gailey. Their higher position made them easily visible above the brush.

"They could cause us trouble," Ben said, frowning. He knew he should have been watching for wild bands instead of thinking. It was only the stallion's strong desire to be with other horses that kept him following them.

"He has stopped!" Andy Blair said, with worry in his voice.

"Keep coming," Ben said. If they stopped, King would have time to consider the situation. Ben increased the gait to a trot, hoping to increase King's fear of being left.

A minute later Andy Blair said, "He's coming. He's coming on now."

Ben did not reply. Dixie still rode beside him, watching the wild horses.

"He's stopped," Andy Blair said again presently. "He's stopped."

"Keep moving," Ben said. If King deserted them for the wild bunch, they would be faced with the task of running him down and Ben had no heart for that—not now.

"He's got his head up," Andy Blair said. "I believe he sees the wild horses."

"Duck into that ravine, Dixie," Ben said, "and ride over and haze those horses out of sight. Drive them back up into one of the canyons. Stay out of King's sight as long as you can. Stay over there to turn him back if he tries to join them. Mr. Blair, you follow me—and keep moving."

A neigh, sustained and eager, sounded behind them, a neigh swelling with fire and life and power, the proud challenge of a wild stallion.

"Ben," Andy Blair said, his voice strong with emotion. "Ben, wait a minute. Wait, Dixie."

"Can't wait," Ben said. "We'll lose him. He'll take off to those other horses. I should have been watching."

"I know," Andy Blair said. "But wait a minute." He pushed his horse into a fast trot, until he rode beside them. "If I bring a couple of good mares up here next spring, will you and Dixie look out for them for me?"

Ben turned in his saddle. "But, why—?" he said.

"Sure we will, Mr. Blair," Dixie said, her voice leaping with new hope. "Sure we will. We'll look after them. We won't let anything happen to them."

"All right," Andy Blair said. "Pull up." He reined his own horse down to a walk and then to a halt.

Ben and Dixie stopped their horses too, and the animals behind them halted. "He'll get away. He'll light out for the wild bunch," Ben told Andy Blair, warningly.

The man shook his head and said, his voice gentle, "He won't get away, not ever—not any more. This is his home; this is where he belongs. It has taken me a long time to realize it, but he never would be happy in a box stall. Even his old sire hated them. He wouldn't be the same horse. I know that now."

"But . . . but," Ben sputtered.

"You're going to let him stay," Dixie cried. "You're going to let him stay up here?"

Andy Blair nodded and said, "If you and Ben will look after him for me."

"We will. Oh, we will!" Dixie said.

Ben was still unable to believe it. "But, what about your colts—the ones you wanted to raise? You wanted Midnight Fire's blood in them?"

"That's the reason I'm going to bring those mares up here," Andy Blair said. "That's just the reason."

A neigh sounded, long and joyous.

"There he goes," Dixie said. "He's made up his mind now."

"Oh, gosh, Mr. Blair," Ben said. "Oh—" His happiness was too great for further words.

The big black horse was moving with long high strides through the brush, head up, mane and tail lifted by the breeze. His eyes were fixed on the wild horses; there was primitive grace and strength in his every movement. And his voice, carrying to them across the rolling brush, was filled with eagerness and lordly challenge.

"That's the blood I want," Andy Blair said. "Wild horse blood."